The Shadow Whisperer

Jennifer S. Hartley

Cover design by Mili Ortiz of Multi Story Media Ltd.
www.multistorymedia.co.uk

ISBN: 9798697771334

PublishNation
www.publishnation.co.uk

In loving memory of my grandfather
Thomas Joseph Hartley
(1907-1973)

Prologue

As a child I used to sleepwalk. As I grew up, they told me I did it less and less until it stopped. Nobody ever realised that the truth was that every day when I awoke the real sleepwalking began. Now I look back desperate to break the habit, desperate to play a waking part in my own life with no idea where to begin and terrified that perhaps it's already too late.

There is a place where angels reside, a place where they meet and discuss their wards, where they seek assistance, where they move to different realms. There is such a place and I know because I walked there. Sometimes I am sure it was nothing but a dream, and other times I know I need that certainty to make sense of all that has happened. So was it a dream? Did I walk with angels and inhabit their world? I don't know. Perhaps I will never know. All I can do is tell you the story and leave it for you to decide.

If we do not learn to tell our stories they will destroy us. I was told that once by a shaman in South America. His words haunted me and I spent the years that followed desperately trying to help others tell their stories, terrified by the idea that our silence could destroy us. It is always easier to help others than to help ourselves and, as they released their stories, I found I could try to forget a little of mine. Forget? No. Then perhaps make peace with it. I showed others how to find their voice and as they did, they released their stories into my keeping. They were horrific stories, so much pain and abuse, so much guilt and torment. I accepted them all. I didn't question. I didn't judge. Yet with each new story I continually pushed my own further and further away. I never quite learned to tell my own story and it remained locked within, as my life drifted by without me ever feeling I was taking an active part in it. I filled the days to help them pass. The fuller they were, the less I needed to think. I would collapse exhausted into bed at night and await the dawn, for this new day to pass so another could come and then another and another until it would all be over. But it became harder and harder to fill that time. Soon even sleep, my sacred escape, began to elude me.

So many of those I have worked with over the years do not initially want to tell their stories. They fear judgement, they fear remembering and, most of all, they fear themselves. There are so many fears to overcome yet fear of telling our story, in essence, is a fear of living. My fear is that my story will disappear within me, swallow me up until I no longer know what happened or did not; where the comedy ended and the tragedy began or was it the other way around? Today as I sit down finally to put pen to paper, I realise that it is not solely my story I will write, not even now. All of our stories are so interwoven and I cannot tell you mine without also sharing the stories of others.

My job has always been to listen to others, to somehow make it easier for them to tell their story and through the telling, to let it go. For a long time this just seemed to happen, people would tell me things and the more we talked the more they would let go of their stories. I thought it was funny at first and my friends and family always laughed at how people were drawn to me in this strange way, offloading their stories then disappearing leaving me with the remnants. When I got older it seemed only natural for it to become my 'work' – yet still I never sought it out. It is important for me that people know that. I *never* went looking for this. Somehow people would find me and share their stories of pain and loss, their traumas, their anger, their fear and shame. They would laugh and cry, some would become enraged screaming at me even though I was blameless. Or was I? And each time I listened to them. I comforted when necessary, encouraged when needed, and accepted the anger and abuse that frequently came with the letting go. What else could I have done? What would you have done in my place?

When people have been quiet for so long, they need to tell their story, they need to pass it on and free themselves. My job is to listen and consume, using one story to help me through the next, to guide me when to speak or even if to speak, to show me how to let it go, lest it should become my own. But is that really possible? I am not so sure anymore. In South America a shaman once explained to me that I was what they called a sin eater. In shamanic tradition a sin eater is called upon by the family of a deceased person to eat a last meal of bread with a sprinkling of salt left on the stomach of the dead as they await burial. Through this ritual it was believed that the sins of that person would be absorbed through the food and they would have clear passage to the afterlife. The sin eater was paid for his or her trouble, but otherwise avoided, feared as being sin-filled and unclean as a result of their work. Those sin eaters usually lived at the edge of the village, unwelcome in the community, and children were warned away from them. In the South American tradition the sin eater is sacred to the society, though never quite a part of it: always needed and respected, but not quite embraced.

Of course my role as a sin eater has a more modern slant. I don't eat off of corpses (honest) and my neighbours and their children do not shun me, as far as I am aware at least. But I serve the purpose of listening to the stories. I listen and then I am dismissed. No longer useful, I serve only as a reminder of the story they wish to move on from. Sometimes people hate those to whom they release their stories because they fear their newfound knowledge and worry that it could be used against them; others despise any reminder of the story which they now feel they have been freed from, leaving it to become the burden of the sin eater

3

alone; and others despise the sin eater for 'making' them tell their story, for drawing out their secrets and magically making them reveal all. Nobody can ever be *made* to tell their story; it is always a choice. It must always be a choice. There is nothing magical in the sin eater's gift, or perhaps curse is a better description, but others find safety in blaming magic and invisible forces when they don't or can't understand and this helps them to alienate the sin eater even more. The more stories you hear, the more you begin to look around and view the world with very different eyes. You become aware of horrors that you never dreamed existed, aware of suffering beyond any you could imagine, you learn the extremities of evil human beings are capable of inflicting on others. It is not that you are shunned by society, but rather that you cease to fit in … if you ever did. Although, if I were being honest, I think you lose any desire to fit into such a world. The knowledge you carry from the stories you have heard makes it all too painful. You become an outcast by your own doing and you live on the edge looking in at everyone else, or out at them. I am never quite sure which of us is the more trapped.

And it was somewhere amongst all of that, I managed to lose both my own story and my identity for a time.

So why was I now sitting in some old woman's kitchen, a woman who told me she spoke to spirits and angels? And how did I come to be in tears as she told me an angel stood behind me with its wings tightly wrapped around me? She told me this angel was trying to comfort me through my pain. And why, I am sure you are wondering, do I believe such things without question or comment? I'm not even sure that the answers are relevant anymore, although I understand why you may want them. All I know is that this day was the culmination of many in which the presence of angels and spirits around me was something of which I was forced to become aware.

But of course all good stories should start at the beginning although I'm not sure where that beginning is. Perhaps I only need to find 'a' beginning and the rest will follow. For so long I have avoided writing all these things down, I have played with them in my head, but they never truly leave me. I guess you can only avoid for so long.

Everything catches up with us eventually.

I

I always felt I would live a life less ordinary. As a child I thought of the things that all children think of (or so my parents tell me) – growing up, marrying, having children, a nice house and a garden – but part of me knew even then that it was never going to happen like that. Part of me recoiled from it and the part that accepted it was bowing down to mere convention. I've never been good at doing what was expected of me – even when I myself have been doing the expecting. Perhaps especially when I have been the one doing the expecting.

I do not believe in death – not as an end. Is it really a question of belief I wonder? I like to see it as a beginning, a difficult beginning perhaps, but a beginning all the same. A difficult end for those left behind, I guess. I do not believe that those we love ever truly leave us. They remain in our memory, in the moments that live on, in the security of a child's hand enfolded in an adult's, in a smile or a wink, in the smell of my grandfather's pipe, or the warmth of a fireplace on a winter's night. They remain and so does the love and so therefore, does the life. And so, I do not believe in death.

"Well death believes in you."

"Should I be expecting it any day soon?" I asked sarcastically.

"Well you should always expect it. An unavoidable certainty for sure. But expecting is not the same as fearing. You took a step towards death the day you were born child. It is all a balancing act. A very fine balancing act." He paused a little too long but just as I was about to fill the silence with my pointless babble, he continued, "We see

ourselves in this solid form, but we are only one percent earth. That means only one percent solidity in each and every atom of our being." Andres stopped, pondering the depth of his own words.

"You've lost me." And not for the first time I considered adding.

"We are more spirit than solidity already." Andres offered by means of an explanation, yet only succeeding in confusing the matter further.

"Is that good or bad? I've got a sneaky feeling it might be bad." I joked dismissively.

"Nothing is good or bad. It simply is." came Andres' somewhat irritating philosophical response. It was yet another unhelpful teaching moment; unhelpful because I had no idea what he was talking about. I wondered if the day would ever come when I understood Andres' riddles. Afterwards I would always try to recall our conversations and write them down meticulously in anticipation that my day of enlightenment might eventually arrive.

I lived abroad for many years and in that time learned much of death in all its forms. Being so far from others, from those you have grown with, from those you love, is a kind of death, an acceptance that the only way to be with those who are so far is in my own mind, my heart, my thoughts and in the words I write. And so began my apprenticeship with death. It is strange but living in that way created in me a fear of owning things. I have a need to be compact in all that I own, never too attached to anything or, it would seem, to anyone. It can all be lost far too easily and attachment to anything is a loss of power, for someone or something can always take it away from you. I have my memories which nobody can ever take from me. And those memories have learned to adapt themselves to my mood, to my desire to remember and, of course, to my need to forget. It is in my mind where I collect the stories and the photographs, the places and the events. They are safe there – at least for now. They travel with me wherever I go. But are our memories true? All I know is they are my truth and that is all I have to work from.

When I returned from those years of living abroad, having died within so many times in those years, I learned of my own death. I returned with my memories of how things had once been and of a girl who had grown into a woman one day and nobody, least of all her, had realised. Few recognised the girl they had once known. So I saw the girl die for the woman to be born in a country where she did not belong and yet was the place they called her 'home', surrounded by people who looked at her with the wary eyes they reserved for foreigners, strangers in their land. I knew that look; it belied every step of acceptance I had strove for in foreign lands. I knew that look because, when I looked in the mirror, a five-year-old stared back at me defiantly with that very same look and with a determination and a sadness beyond her years.

I have always been a foreigner in a strange land and my only grounding has always been my words, words written and unread that fall on deaf ears, read by blind eyes across oceans and continents. What makes a writer a writer? When I was five years old I announced to the world - via my family - that I was going to be a writer. They looked at me somewhat concerned, they had been hoping for something more realistic perhaps, like a princess or a fairy. Clearly I was out to disappoint and after the shadow incident this was almost too much. The shadow incident - another story that will only keep me from my point so I will pass it by, for the moment at least. The shadow…it is a story like so many others that stick in my mind with a clarity that is almost cruel: a moment in childhood when we are forced to see with adult eyes. Moments that can never be returned. Moments when we should be left well alone in that sacred space where we know that imaginary friends are real and angels sit on our shoulders and whisper in our ears, kissing the strands of our hair that blow in the wind. Sometimes, on good days, I think I still hear those whispers and feel the gentle kisses and I reach out my hand and grasp at the air and hear their laughter as they run to join the shadows in a world that exists astride mine.

"What are you going to write?" they asked with what I now know to be cynicism, or is it scepticism?

"I don't know." I replied a little bemused at the stupidity and pointlessness of the question. "I just know I have something to say." And everyone laughed, including me. I don't think any of us knew what was funny about that, I only knew I didn't care and that in itself was quite funny for a five-year-old whose family and teachers worried was psychologically damaged from the sudden death of her grandfather. Well of course I was damaged! My period of perfection in another's eyes had come to an end. From that point on I had to learn to see myself through my own eyes instead of those of my grandfather, and what I saw was destined never to be quite as wonderful or beautiful. Once again, I am getting ahead of myself. I find the intricate web our memories spin always disrupts my attempts at any form of linear flow.

What makes a writer a writer? It is not training nor education nor practise – they are merely tools to sharpen the gift. What makes a writer a writer? It is a birth right, a gift and a curse, the extremity of all extremities, the secret key to a world beyond that in which we live, a world of imagination and dreams that knows no bounds; a world with the ability to delight and destroy, to raise and break the spirit with the spilling of ink. That is the world I walk astride; the world I have always walked astride and always will. But the gift of storytelling was given to me with the curse of the sin eater as the shamans called it. The one to whom others would come to unburden themselves of their stories, their sins; the one who would hear the stories no one else should ever have to; the one who would write them down to preserve the memories of others. So to become a teller of stories, I first had to become a listener to stories. Never allowed to choose those I would hear or the people who would come to me. It was a steep price to pay. That has been my right of passage. All gifts are curses and all curses are gifts, perhaps all it depends on is a slant of the eye, a tilt of the head. How we choose to view things, I have learned, is often what decides our fate.

"I've had enough! I screamed. I'm sick of eating sins. I can't do it anymore. I'm sick! Sick!" I repeated the word for emphasis and to hide, unsuccessfully, the fact that my voice was becoming a screech as it always did when I got upset. Andres laughed. "Don't laugh at me Andres. I don't want this. I can't do it anymore."

"You have no choice."

"Yes I do, damn you! Of course I do." I replied indignant that he had dared to say I had no choice.

"You accepted it."

"Hardly! I don't remember being given a choice. I don't recall applying for the position. I don't remember filling out some bloody form to allow spirits to come in and out of my head, or to eat dead people's sins! Do you? Well do you?" I paused before continuing in a calmer voice, "Andres I don't even understand any of this."

"You understand what you need to understand for the moment. You chose it because you sought it, perhaps not consciously, but you sought it. A glimpse into the eternity of our existence is a gift mi hija."

"Is that supposed to help? Damn you Andres, you and your philosophical shit? Damn you! Just close my head or whatever it is you need to do." Andres chuckled quietly and in his calm unfaltering voice replied, "But, mi hija, you and I both know it's too late for that. It was always too late." I opened my mouth but could say nothing, my mind was

trying to block him out, block it all out. "Maya it was always too late." He repeated for emphasis. I wanted to make some smart comment – as I always do - about how I would defy them all by becoming the first ever anorexic sin eater, but nothing came out of my mouth but a choking sound as I realised I was about to cry.

"There's no turning back is there?" Even as I asked the question, I already knew the answer. There had never been a way to turn back.

"Mi hija, what would we turn back to?"

"A time when I was not a sin eater?" It was a statement posed as a question but deep down I knew there had never been such a time, though I could not bring myself to say that, to acknowledge the truth of it. I knew it in my heart and Andres knew it too. I slid down the wall and slumped to the ground fighting back tears of frustration, anger and confusion.

"There is just so much I don't understand Andres."

"Why do you need to understand?"

"I don't know where I am going, that's why. I don't know what I'm doing anymore"

"Mi hija you've always known where you were going, I've rarely met anyone with such certainty." Andres chuckled.

"Certainty! Certainty! Andres don't be so ridiculous! The only certainty in my life is the ongoing uncertainty."

"Exactly! Your certainty was in the journey." He smiled that calm unruffled smile of the wise who always know more than they say. I was infuriated.

"Is that supposed to help?" I could hear my voice beginning to rise again.

"It's time to stop fighting. There is so much love and support available to you if you just let it in. And, by the way, you and I both know it's the uncertainty that you love. Don't kid yourself that it is not the case."

12

"Perhaps it was at one time, yes perhaps that is true, but not now.... The adventures, the stories...The sins I gorge myself on. Just as well those sins have no calorie count."

Andres smiled, "Your jokes betray you mi hija and, forgive me for saying so, but they are never funny. You think that if you frighten people away, you can avoid being hurt even more than you have already. But it does not work like that, you are just preventing the healing process from taking its course."

"Go to hell!"

Andres laughed again. "I've already been. Don't we all go there sooner or later, in one form or another? But we don't all get to return. You are one of the lucky ones, and you know it. I think perhaps you need to remind yourself of that and to be more grateful."

"I didn't think you believed in luck."

"I don't. But I like the sound of the word."

We both smiled. "Tell me what you see Andres, please."

"Why? Wouldn't you prefer the surprise?"

"I've had enough surprises to last me a lifetime thank you very much!"

"Enjoy what lies ahead, enjoy not knowing. It is good."

"Good! Is that good in some mystical sense that would mean bad to every other sane person in the world? Cos I'd really like some earthly grounded good in my life for a change and no more cryptic spiritual messages please."

"I didn't know you knew so many sane people, actually I didn't know you knew any." He was cheekily, softening his sarcasm in the process. "Having nothing to hold on to, no sense of direction, no idea of the choices and possibilities that might lie ahead, it's scary but it is also exciting. It all depends on your point of view. Relax and let what will come, come. A clear understanding will bring clear expectations. You are stronger than you realise. But everything has its price mi hija." I looked at him unaware that I was even crying until he handed me a handkerchief.

13

"You have to stop running away from who you are, from what you are, from what you are meant to be and do. So much energy used up in running all the time, never stopping. Learn to embrace it. Resistance will not make it go away." He walked around the room slowly, his head bowed and his hands clasped loosely behind his back. He thought for some time before he spoke again deliberately enunciating each word, *"Mi hija, do you believe in God?"* The shift in his thought process caught me by surprise, not for the first time. It was a statement more than a question but he looked at me clearly expecting a response.

"Yes Andres I believe in God. But I am just not so sure that He believes in me."

"Oh He does, He does!" Andres chuckled to himself, clearly amused by my response, *"Although I am sure you never make it easy for Him. God never stopped believing in you, you stopped believing in yourself. I have protected you from evil, from the spirits that tried to destroy you, from the people who tried to hurt you. And although I have tried mi hija, I cannot protect you from yourself. You are your own worst enemy."* How often had I heard those words I thought? *"You have a light that is so strong you can pull people towards you, but that strength, that light is matched by an incredible negativity that you must learn to master or it will destroy you. There are more gifts that you still have to realise."*

"No thank you! Sin eating is more than enough for me Andres!"

"Tell me, if you could change it all, not know the truth, not have heard all the stories, eaten all the sins, would you – tell me truly – would you change it mi hija? Have it never have happened, none of it?"

"No. No I wouldn't change it." I surprised myself at how certainly and quickly I responded.

"Why?"

"Because ... who else would do it?"

14

He put his hand on my shoulder and looked at me, shaking his head. *"You have made enough offerings, there is no need to make any more. The spirits want you to know this."*

"Does that mean I've earned the right to close my head?" I asked hopefully.

"We both know that will never happen." Andres replied laughing.

It was worth a try I thought, knowing he would hear. I would not change it Andres. I would not change any of it. I stood up to leave but turned back to look at him as I reached the door. *"But it is hard Andres and I don't know what to do at times. I don't know if I even can do it at times. There are some stories I wish I had never heard; sins I do not know how to digest. And what if I can't? What if the stories stay with me forever?"*

He looked at me nodding his head. *"I know, I know. But remember the young woman I met all those years ago and look at you now. You have much to be proud of, so very much."* Then he turned back to concentrate on his shells and stones, oblivious to the fact that I remained standing there waiting for some words of wisdom that would miraculously make it all okay, words that never came.

All those years ago he had said. It seemed like another lifetime ago now. Thinking back on how we met made me laugh out loud. So how then had it come to this?

II

We all deserve, at least once in our lives, to have someone love us so much that we are perfect to them. A love that can only see all that is good and beautiful in us and is blind to all our imperfections. For me that person was my grandfather and although he died exactly two months before my fifth birthday, he left an indelible mark, a memory that has never left me; a memory that grew with me. I miss him as much, if not more, today than I did the day I was told he had died. How is it possible to miss someone so much when you only knew them for a fraction of your life?

I was a difficult child in many ways – not perhaps the most obvious. I could sit quietly playing for hours on end and often required little attention, but I was headstrong and direct even as a small child, precocious in my independence and intolerant of my perceived weakness in others. My grandfather saw beauty and perfection and very little else – even my faults were somehow justifiable and it soon became clear that I was calling the shots in our relationship. This was a large well-built World War II veteran, a man's man who smoked and drank and cursed like the sailor he had been, he was not the family type and he was certainly not one to be manipulated by anyone, unless of course that person happened to be me. For some reason he changed with me, and the man I knew was only ever soft, gentle and loving; a man I could wrap around my little finger to get whatever I wanted; a man who made me feel safe in a way I have never felt since losing him; a man who made me believe everything would always work out just fine in the end and I would always be safe and happy.

He would take the long bus ride to our home early every morning and leave after dinner. My sister would go to school, my parents to work and their studies, and he and I would remain in our own world of imagined princesses and adventure, of chocolate cake and pie with chips. He never scolded, never shouted, even when I deserved that and more. For me, and me alone, his patience knew no limits. Then one day he became ill. There was no warning it was coming, literally it appeared he was fine one day and not the next. He had been in pain for a long time and dismissed it as the result of an old war wound, but as the pain increased so too did his concern and finally, he surrendered to the doctor's pleas and went to hospital for some tests. Two weeks later my grandfather was dead from a cancer that had been spreading throughout his body for months. There had been no warning, no time to prepare, barely time for the adults around me to digest the information. Nobody told me what was happening and I was far too young to understand the gravity of the situation as it unfolded.

I remember as clearly as if it had just happened yesterday, that my sister, mother and I went shopping for new shoes in the city centre on a Saturday afternoon. For some reason my mother relented and allowed me to buy red shoes I was demanding in preparation for starting school. She didn't try to fight my determination not to get the sensible black school ones she had told me I must have. We went from there to the hospital and I ran down the ward to my grandfather's bed excited and happy to show him my shiny new red shoes with their fancy double buckle. I climbed up on the bed thrusting the shoes in his face and he lay there barely moving, showing little interest. I was hurt and angry, I couldn't understand why the man who always had time for me was so disinterested all of a sudden in something so important (in my mind at least) and I insisted relentlessly that I was bored and I wanted to go home. Eventually my mother, weary of my complaining, gave in and we left. I ran down the hospital ward, desperate to get out of there and home so I could put on my beautiful new shoes. I was just a child and by the time we had reached home I had forgotten all about my grandfather's apparent disinterest. In my head I believed I would see him in a couple of days and all would be back to normal. Few children hold grudges, it is very much an adult behaviour. It is strange though how some memories live on in us no matter how hard we try to forget. That day is a memory I have longed to forget for most of my life. The more I try to forget, the sharper the memory becomes.

That night my father went to the hospital to visit my grandpa, returning after our bedtime. We were still awake and could hear some kind of discussion in the hallway. Suddenly my father opened our bedroom door and informed us that my grandfather was dead and then left again closing the door behind him. My father was obviously consumed by his own grief and trying to protect us from seeing him upset. He was trying to process the sudden and painful loss of a parent and all that would come with it. I was just a child but I knew dead meant my grandpa was never coming back, that I would never see him again and suddenly, with that realisation, my world came crashing down around me. I didn't cry, the pain was too immense. I have since come to understand that sorrow and pain can bring an emotion beyond expression, beyond tears. I remember lying on my bed looking out of the window at the night sky. I had the most terrible pain in my heart and my head was spinning and as I finally closed my eyes it was in the knowledge that this pain meant my heart had physically broken and so I too would now die and be with my grandpa. I knew this and I was fine with it, death would stop the pain and the emptiness; death would mean I didn't have to try to go on without the love and protection of my grandpa. The next morning however I awoke.

It is a harsh lesson to learn so young that life goes on regardless of our own personal pain and suffering. Most of us are given more time in naïve existence before facing such a reality. But my grandfather's death came to mean so much more in my life. As a child I decided I could never allow myself to love someone so much ever again; that I could never afford to damage a heart that was already now broken. I truly believed any more pain would irreparably damage what was left of my fragile heart. I also decided that I would learn how to be so strong that I would never need anyone else to take care of or help me. I was well into my adult years before it ever occurred to me that these were odd decisions for a young child to make. I also realised that the path my life was on changed the day my grandfather died. Often I have wondered about the life I would have led had he lived longer. And I know my life would have turned out very differently had he lived; I would have turned out very differently. That is something I have thought about a lot, his death had such a profound effect on me, my outlook on life and feelings towards attachment that have affected the adult I have become in every way. Sometimes it's hard to imagine a different 'me' but then I remember that child, almost five years old, and know I wasn't always so difficult, so hard and so closed off to allowing people into my life.

My parents never told me about the funeral. They thought it best I didn't go. After all, they said, I didn't really understand what was happening. And so my last memory of my grandfather is him lying in that hospital bed and me complaining that I wanted to go home. I never wore those red shoes. I refused to put them on or even look at them again. My parents, dealing with their own grief, chose not to fight me over the issue although I don't think they ever understood why I hated those shoes so much. I never got to say goodbye to my grandfather. I never got to say sorry for that day at the hospital and the child's guilt and pain was carried well into adulthood. The adult in me rationalises all of this a great deal but the child clings to it with a ferocious tenacity. The adult in me begs forgiveness from him every day even though I know he would say there is nothing to forgive. Sometimes I think about the pain my grandfather must have been in for so long. He never complained or said anything so that he could maintain his commitment to looking after me every day. How my heart aches when I think about that. Only recently did I realise that the greatest pain I feel is not that my grandfather left me, but that he never took me with him.

A few weeks later I was playing alone at school. I was not excluded from the other children and their games but sometimes, even then, I needed space to be on my own, with my own ideas. Time to be with the angels who kept me company and with whom I spoke. Why do we fear so greatly the psychic awareness of children? Why are we afraid of and so quick to dismiss the possibility that they freely see spirits? It is such a beautiful gift that gets knocked out of us at a young age, when we are told that the spirits we see are a part of our imagination, that they do not exist in reality. And with time we come to believe that must be the truth and with the loss of the belief comes the loss of the gift. And it is a gift – one of the most beautiful gifts granted to us. In my case, I may have stopped seeing for a time but I never stopped believing and so I never stopped sensing. Perhaps that would explain all that happened later, what Andres and the others tried to explain to me.

This particular day was one of the last days of autumn, a beautiful sunny day. Those days that combine a cold air with bright sunshine, when everything feels crisp and alive. As I stood in the crowded playground, I became acutely aware of my shadow and she became acutely aware of me. I bent to the ground eager to touch her head, yet each time I bent down and stretched out my hand, she grew far out of my reach. We began a game of tag together. I was convinced if I could just be that little bit faster, I would catch her and the thought made me giggle with delight. I tried over and over again, amazed by her ability to beat me every time. I tried to jump down quicker and catch her unawares, but each time she managed to slip from my reach. I was so engrossed in this wonderful game that I failed to hear the bell calling us to form a line and return to class. I failed to see all the children line up awaiting their teacher, ready to enter the building. I failed to hear the teacher calling to me. I did not however fail to hear the laughter of the other children as they all turned around to watch me.

There are some moments in our lives when, no matter how young we may be, we realise that we have failed to fit in, realise that something makes us different and no matter how creative or beautiful that thing may be, it is frowned on and rejected by others. What I was doing made the most perfect sense to a child about to turn five, there was certainly nothing *wrong* in what I was doing, nothing abnormal. My crime was that I wasn't doing what the other children were doing. By not doing what I was expected to do, I was in the wrong. Something that seems to have followed me throughout my life.

In the days that followed at every break all the children in my class were reminded to play together, to include *everybody* in their games. And in those looks and innuendos I quickly learned shame though I didn't understand what I had done to justify it. I learned that I should not act differently, that I should not stand out, that I should never draw attention to myself. My parents were contacted and I learned that I had also caused them to worry by acting in this way, though I still did not understand why. The school asked if there were problems at home, if there were any problems with me. The truth is that the only problem was that I was trying to be a child in an adult world; a world that defines its children by adult standards.

Another lesson learned, that has served me well in the future events that came to pass, was that what we can see and hear, what we can feel and sense, are sometimes better kept to ourselves; that anything that marks us as different often equally marks us as a threat. At five years old I represented a threat to the standard acceptable behaviour that tells us to ensure we do not stand out from the crowd in any way.

We all deserve, at least once in our lives, to have someone love us so much that we are perfect for them. A love that can only see all that is good and beautiful in us and is blind to all our imperfections. For me that person was my grandfather. He died two months to the day before my fifth birthday...but existence is continuous, it is a continuum and so there is no death, only new beginnings. How can life die?

"When does a thought become bad Andres?"

"When we start thinking it." He smiled, "You think too much Maya, that is not good."

"Things will get better, the sadness and disappointment that feels like it is overwhelming me will pass, wont it?" I wasn't sure if I was asking or begging.

"It always does." came the simple reply.

"But that's what makes it so much more painful. I am sick and tired of making it through each disappointment. I want things not to be so hard." I turned on Andres with such anger though it was never directed at him. "I want to be loved and accepted for who I am and not feel like I always fall short."

"Fall short of what? Who is it that does not accept you? Can you not see that it is you yourself?"

" It seems I want too much."

"Stop running and the frustration will cease. Stop running and turn inwards. Then you will smile, life is so entertaining when we stop running from it."

"More riddles Andres."

"You say riddles, I say wisdom. Who knows? Your wisdom sounds like riddles to me." He chuckled at his own joke and as I opened my mouth to speak, I realised I too was smiling.

"I guess we don't make much sense to one another at times."

"Two negatives make a positive – we make perfect sense mi hija, we just don't always understand it."

"Why do you insist on calling 'mi hija' (my child)? I am not a child. Is it to remind me of my ignorance, my naivety?"

"To remind you of your innocence, to remind you not to forget that child who lost her shadow so many years ago."

"How did you know, I never told you about that...?"

"How did I know what? I look at you and see no shadow so I know you must have lost it. Only children lose their shadows. Perhaps you lost it through carelessness. Perhaps you haven't been looking for it in the right places. Now I need to work and you need to go. No more questions because..."

"There are no answers!" And we laughed. I didn't need to ask how he knew about the shadow. He just did and that was all that was important.

But had I really lost my shadow? Did she run away in shame on that sunny autumn day when everyone had laughed at me?

"Where do I look for a missing shadow Andres?"

"In the light of course." Replied Andres laughing.

In the background I can hear the piano music I always listen to when I am writing. Music that makes me feel someone else understood this kind of pain, these thoughts. And yes, I will go on and yes, I will be stronger for it but the truth is I no longer feel I want to go on and I don't need more strength. Andres how am I supposed to evolve? Where do I go from here? Those were the questions I wanted to ask but didn't. Why? Part of me feared Andres would tell me to look within for the answers; a greater part of me feared he would tell me the answer.

III

Are the waves of Samsara washing over me or drowning me? I've been trying to work this out, trying to decide what the hell I am going to do next. Knowing that with each passing day I am recognising not only how temporary a being I am but also how short this lifetime is. There is so much to do and so little time in which to complete all that needs done. Or is my current completion to reach the beginning? I am in one of those moods – they make me sound good, but even I rarely know what I am talking about. It impresses people though – they think I'm 'deep' which is my ideal cover for being antisocial.

Since I was a child I knew two things for certain: I was a writer and I was a Catholic. The first I seemed to know instinctively, the second I had instilled in me. I'm not sure which I've struggled with most, all I know is they have both plagued me throughout my life and every time I try to ignore one, it always seems to come back to haunt me.

With little else to do and in an attempt to avoid thinking about anything too serious or meaningful in my existence, I have been thinking a lot about religion. Who does that? People turn to religion for meaning, whereas I turned to it to avoid finding meaning. You need to understand religion has never come easy to me. Spirituality I can embrace with all my being and beyond – organised religion I cannot. Perhaps I just want to be a supermarket Catholic or Buddhist or whatever, selecting the things that appeal to me most in order to formulate some exotic (aka convenient) combination that I can live by. Although I doubt that is true because I detest labels of any kind. Perhaps I am simply too judgmental. I don't like someone judging me to be a good or bad person, moral or immoral based on my religious tendencies (or, to be more precise, my lack of them), as they can certainly be very misleading. I realise my insistence on being non-judgmental makes me the judgmental one! Why is nothing simple?

Being brought up a Catholic, and strictly so, ensured being brought up with a strong, if not over-developed, sense of guilt. Never quite sure what I was guilty of, I can only identify with a comment the writer Graham Greene made in one of his novels about how Catholics are doomed by their knowledge. We know too much about sin and, more significantly, its repercussions. Innocent pleasures come laced with guilt, simple questions inevitably turn into philosophical debates and we learn the skills of 'judgementalism' while being taught how to have a 'Christian' open mind. My life, my very existence, is wrought with contradictions.

While I could never reject Catholicism, I discovered that it could reject me, judging me unfit in my interpretation of its laws and guidelines. But that has not and never will stop me. Like alcoholism, once a Catholic always a Catholic no matter what steps I may take to recovery! And trust me I've tried many. I am who I am and, within that context, I aim to live as good a life as I can, but so many things just seem to get in the way. Will God not love me at least for trying? Don't they say everyone loves a trier? He should definitely take pity on me for my poor attempts. Will He not judge foremost what was in my heart? And does He not also think that the Catholic church is wrong at times, after all history does quite literally speak volumes on this? I detest being labelled a spiritual tourist. Although the word tourist implies an element of fun and I certainly seem to have missed that part. While I have dabbled in a variety of spiritual beliefs, I have never sought to abandon my basic (or inherent) Catholicism, but rather to compliment it. Perhaps that is not so true, I wanted to adapt it. I wanted my own version of Catholicism based on a set of rules that worked for me.

My parents belonged to various church groups over the years, but as a child the one I remember most was The Legion of Mary. Probably because it was the first group they joined with their newfound, or rather newly intensified faith. It is a lay apostolic association of Catholics worldwide who, with the sanction of the Church and under the leadership of the Virgin Mary (in spirit I assume as she never attended any of the meetings I went to), serve the Church and their communities. My parents were members and so my sister and I were taken to meetings and also became members in a manner of speaking. I guess it was more economical than paying a babysitter. It was the first but by no means last church organisation I became a part of during my childhood. At the time most of it seemed natural but as I reached my teens I rebelled, especially on realising none of my friends were part of such groups. In my teens I felt embarrassed by my parents' religious fervour and I also lacked any understanding of why I was a part of it, outside of it being the will of my parents. I wanted to make my own choices and find my own way on my own spiritual path, I guess. Little did I know what the years ahead were about to bring. A great lesson on the wisdom of the saying, 'be careful what you wish for'.

Our being a part of the Legion of Mary group boosted the group's numbers significantly. My fondest memory of this pious period of my life was being made the group's treasurer. Not to be self-deprecating but this was not a wise choice on behalf of the group and undoubtedly not one they would class as a fond memory. Unfortunately the funds decreased under my guard with me spending a great deal of it (needless to say not on religious artefacts) and being promptly demoted to the room organiser (setting out the chairs!). I feel the need to clarify that we are talking minimal takings here, not some million-dollar heist.

Actually that reminds me of a similar incident which I realise is not painting me in the best of lights. However I do not consider myself a thief, more a sort of modern-day Robin Hood. I was stealing from the rich in a manner of speaking – the church – in order to give to the poor – and that would be me.

Every Christmas throughout my childhood my father, with others, set up a large nativity scene in the local shopping mall. It was a crib with giant painted statues, set in a large barn scene with a painted background of Bethlehem. The idea being to remind people of the true meaning of Christmas. Willing volunteers and me (who neither volunteered nor was willing) would take turns standing at the crib and handing out prayer leaflets to what I can only describe as extremely disinterested passers-by. This was our local mall and it was Christmas time, meaning almost everyone I knew from school was passing the crib at some point. The unlucky days it fell on me to hand out the leaflets and preach the word of God was usually a weekend when there was no school. I was there for all to see and it quickly became a point of ridicule in school the following Monday. I tried to hide every time I saw someone I knew approaching the crib. I'd run around the side crouching behind a statue of a shepherd or a cow while praying to little Baby Jesus to give me the gift of invisibility. My prayers fell on deaf ears and inevitably I was seen year in, year out. I felt humiliated and angered by the whole situation, though unsure why or who to direct my anger at. And so it rapidly became directed at Baby Jesus and I quickly found the perfect way to get my revenge.

At the front of the crib was a donations box and each day my father would collect it and each day the money would be counted, bagged and then banked. Now this I did volunteer for. As the money was bagged, I would put five bags to one side for Baby Jesus and one to the other side (and in my backpack where nobody could see) for Maya.

Over the years the ratio may have changed more in my favour but there's no need for us to go into that now...or ever for that matter. I felt if that if I were being made to work then why shouldn't I be paid for it? Did I not deserve it? It wasn't stealing. It was payment for enforced child labour!

It's strange but a couple of years ago I walked through that mall at Christmas and I couldn't find the crib anywhere. I felt sad, as if something had been lost from my childhood. As I wandered around, I finally found the 'new' nativity scene, tucked away at the end of the food court where few people ever passed by. It was no longer formed from the carefully painted statues. Instead shop mannequins, poorly put together and dressed in a rushed and careless manner had been placed precariously on a pile of hay. The scene was simultaneously funny and sad.

Joseph was a black mannequin with a white arm, while Mary had two left hands. They had clearly failed to obtain a baby mannequin for Jesus, so instead had cut out a picture of a baby's face and stuck it on a pillow. A blanket covering where His body should be did not quite reach his head, making it look like He had been decapitated. There was a mannequin dressed as an angel hovering above the scene supported by a wire. However the wire had been placed too far down her body making her top heavy. The result being that she looked like she was diving in for an attack on the Baby Jesus. Her blonde curly wig had also fallen as a result of her precarious angle and was now draped over what was supposed to be a cow. The three shepherds looked like they were recovering from a heavy night's drinking as they had been propped up against the wall. There was only one king – he'd obviously lost his two friends en route. Clearly he had also taken advantage of the pre-Christmas sales and was sporting a new pair of Nike trainers. Not for long I couldn't help thinking. The guiding star had clearly not responded well to various attempts to stick it to the

29

backdrop (clear from the multiple glue stains) and so someone had instead stabbed it into a helpless sheep in the corner. I wondered if Baby Jesus would see the funny side to it all. It seemed like nobody cared anymore and I felt incredibly saddened by the ridiculous scene and the clearly forgotten message of Christmas. I sat with a coffee in a café opposite and watched people walk past. Few even cast a glance at the crib, almost nobody stopped and those who did mocked the poor and effortless set up.

Anyway, returning to my Legion of Mary days, another memory that I find utterly horrific today, yet one I accepted as part of my disturbing/disturbed normality in my childhood, was my Jehovah Witness style going round the doors! One of our duties was to go to the houses of good Catholic families in our neighbourhood convincing them to take in the statue of the Virgin Mary for a week and say a novena while giving her a home (or something like that, I never paid much attention). All the old people would usually feel sorry for us (who could blame them) and give us tea and biscuits. They were probably grateful for the company and someone to speak to and we were grateful for the tea and biscuits. Often, we wouldn't knock on the doors (my idea) and go home to tell my father that nobody was in, but he caught on quickly as frequently and suspiciously everyone was out each time my sister and I did the rounds. Then of course my sister would always snitch on me, telling my father how I had forced her to lie and pretend nobody was in. My sister, though older, was always the good one. She never challenged my parents' rules and rarely did anything wrong. Her obedience and commendable behaviour made me look like I had been spawned by the devil. This resulted in me frequently being told how 'difficult' I was. Whether it be my parents, teachers, other family members, I was constantly described as a 'difficult' child. This enraged me and so I found myself growing into being the 'difficult' teenager. My logic was that if everyone wanted to call me difficult, then I would oblige and ensure I was. And I did. As I reached adulthood, I found I frequently forewarned others by describing myself as 'difficult'. I had taken on the label and all the baggage that came with it.

I should point out regarding the going round doors that these were different times. I can't imagine anyone allowing their child to knock on strangers' doors and enter their house in the name of God these days. Although come to think of it the world was full of psychopaths and paedophiles then too, we just weren't as aware and clearly were a hell of a lot more trusting. We never went to random doors, they were all registered parishioners – not that that is any assurance they weren't criminals. I never felt unsafe though, just somewhat humiliated at going through the process. How I ever survived high school I will never know. I somehow scraped through without becoming a complete outcast. I was certainly not the most popular kid, but I was also far from the strangest kid at school, which may say more about the school than me. I worked desperately hard to hide my extra-curricular religious activities and was adept at lying, a skill I thank God for, quite literally. Had He not created so many situations I had to lie about; I would never have got quite so good at lying in the first place. God made me a compulsive liar!

Then there were the prayer nights at chapel when my mother would encouragingly ask, "Would you like to lead us in prayer tonight Maya?" and I would reply screwing my face up in horror as if my mother had sprouted a second head, "No!" "Not to worry, perhaps another night then." And with that a third head appeared! My parents never understood that any chance of me ever being one of the cool kids was destroyed completely by their religious ferocity and also the fact that they made me wear terribly sensible shoes and a duffel coat (before they became a fashion statement). There was of course also the small issue of my

31

father touring the Catholic schools giving talks and a slide show on the Virgin Mary and how we were all going to hell if we didn't say our prayers! Hell here I come! People have ended up in a psychologist's chair for less! Yet looking back I actually find it all quite funny though I couldn't begin to tell you why. At the time I resented my parents, but now I feel immensely grateful for my upbringing.

For some reason throughout a large part of the years after I left home, I went in search of what I thought was God, my religion, my spirituality. It was years before I realised that I was simply searching for me. Had I realised earlier it would have been so much easier, though infinitely less eventful. I quickly learned that various spiritual paths all attract their 'types'. Anyway Zen and a couple of Shamanic journeys later (to mention just a few of my spiritual ventures) I found myself one fine blustery winter's evening studying meditation techniques under the auspices of Tibetan Buddhism. I have no doubt that all faiths have an incredible amount in common and that ultimately, we really are all worshipping the same God, with the odd variation here and there for good measure. How we all go about it, interpreting the finer details, is where the differences creep in. But what I have learned is that when a group get together for any religious or spiritual reasons, their basic formation is almost always the same.

Every group I have attended since and including the Legion of Mary, seemed to be made up of the same ingredients. There will be someone who is dying, someone lost, someone recovering from an addiction, someone in full thrust of an addiction, someone who thinks they have been spiritually reborn (and takes it upon themselves to try to force the rest of the world to be reborn with them), someone who thinks they are on another level of spiritual superiority, someone who is overly analytical, another overly emotional, another overly intellectual, someone who is mad and someone who came by mistake thinking it was

32

something else (actually the Legion of Mary didn't have that many people in it come to think of it). Then, of course, there is me. Although some might argue that I could quite easily fit into one or more of the above categories.

Buddhist, Catholic, whatever the group, they are drawn to one another in this formation and I sit on the outside looking in (or is it vice versa?), suspiciously eyed as if I were a spy, pitied and envied simultaneously. They never seem sure if it is I who knows something they don't, or the other way around. I've never been sure myself. As meetings go however, I must point out that the Buddhists always seem to provide the best tea (not just your normal bog-standard type) and delicious biscuits. Can faith be bought? If so, mine is apparently going quite cheap!

The attraction of meditation, if not Buddhism, was immense. To find peace in my own mind, my own being – to strengthen my resolve in the face of adversity ... who could resist? Are we not all searching for that seemingly ungraspable inner peace? But everything comes in a package and the deeper we go into it the more layers that need unwrapping. Within that the Buddhist notion/belief of loving all sentient beings proved a complex issue. How can I possibly love all humans and animals and insects? Why in God's name would I even want to? Or am I missing the point? Of course I am missing the point, usually deliberately. The art of avoidance, keeping everyone at arm's length. I wanted to know this inner peace because I felt I had never had it. As if my head had been in a swirl since the day I was born. A swirl would have been better than the truth that was awaiting me.

"It is not a curse." Andres was becoming irritated by my stubbornness, though as always he attempted to hide it.
"It feels like it."
"Perspective."
"I have none."

"Well we can finally agree." Andres laughed at his own joke, that hearty laugh which he seemed to enjoy in its own right, regardless of whether he laughed alone or not. He continued, "You must remember the story of Socrates three gates before you speak."

"Must I?" I replied sarcastically. "And what would that be?"

"Before speaking your words should pass through three gates. If they cannot pass through those gates, they are words that should never be spoken. First you must ask: is what I am about to say true? If so then comes second question: is what I am about to say kind? If so, you now arrive at the final question: is what I am about to say necessary? Only then should you speak."

"I think I may never speak again if I'm following that criteria! I should have been born mute!"

"That would be a blessing to us all mi hija." Andres replied mockingly.

"I'm cursed Andres. My life is one big curse." I complained dramatically like a spoiled child.

"You know better than most what it truly means to be cursed mi hija," Andres replied in gentle reproach. "You should not make such comments."

"The chickens?"

"The chickens."

We both looked at one another and burst out laughing. Time certainly has a wonderful way of changing how we view past incidents. For such a long time I never thought I'd be able to laugh about the chickens.

IV

I say it all began a few years ago but if I were being honest, I think it truly began long before that. But the last few years have been the catalyst. If you had asked me even just a few years ago if I believed in spirits and spells, in mystical gifts and deep-set curses, I would have laughed dismissively. If you asked me today what I believe I could not answer. All I can tell you is that I have learned in these years not to disbelieve. There are things, so many things, I cannot explain with logic and reason. I wish I could. There are things I have seen that if I tell others they would laugh at me disbelievingly or think I was mad. But I don't need others to believe what has happened to me over the years. There was a time when I did, but that was more of a hope, I think. A hope that their disbelief could make it all unreal for me too, that it was all just the product of an overactive imagination. Now I accept it and talk about it to few and have ceased to disbelieve in a world I fail to understand. A world I am often not sure I even want to understand or need to for that matter. Understanding is highly overrated I have discovered. So why am I telling you this now? Why am I writing it down, risking being laughed at, disbelieved and dismissed? Fear I think. Fear that all the stories that led me to where I am now will be lost in the depths of my own mind. Fear that my own story will overwhelm me. Fear that my story will destroy me or disappear like the burning embers of a fire.

It was 1996 when I first had my crude initiation into the world of spirits. When I say crude it would be more accurate and honest to say ridiculous. I look back on it and laugh at myself, my ignorance and my incredible naivety. It was a new and different experience that I thought I would embark on... that's a lie. I had no intention or desire to embark on the experience. I was not given a choice. I thought it would be over quickly and normality would return. I believed it would be my secret and nobody need ever know. I was wrong on every possible count. Despite that I remember my initiation into this magical world fondly now for it always makes me laugh and laughter is necessary when you are dealing with these things, believe me.

I had been living in South America for a couple of years, a strange experience in itself. I was living in a country called Arajua, derogatively referred to as the arm pit of South America. If you go there you will understand why. I'm clearly not doing their tourist industry any favours. Don't get me wrong, I love that country. The problem is that I hate and love it in equal measure, and it feels the same about me. Perhaps that is the real problem. I may be flattering or deluding myself as I think the hate Arajua feels towards me probably outweighs the love in the end.

Its geographical position tucks it inland to the west surrounded by Chile, Bolivia and Peru. It is a country of extremes, a land rich in resources yet less than a third of it is inhabited or, to be more accurate, habitable. There is rarely a midpoint living there and the only one that comes to mind is the Río Arajua, the great river that divides the country geographically. It was one of the first South American countries to achieve autonomy from the Spaniards and ironically it has been one of the least free ever since. To any outsider the country appears to be caught in a time warp, even in the capital Coronación, the most developed city in the country. The majority of buildings in the city centre are colonial in style, dilapidated, unpreserved and uncared for; the buses, aged and battered, are constantly breaking down; tram lines are overgrown with moss and shrubbery; there are few modern buildings with the exception of the more recent suburban developments; there are no skyscrapers. The city centre bears witness to a mixture of cultural groups rejected by Arajua's 'modern' society such as the colourful yet impoverished sight of the Indigenous Arajuani who populate the main plaza daily in an attempt to sell their handicrafts; or the despised Mennonite groups who appear a couple of times a week from the interior to sell their cheese and butter and buy supplies before rapidly returning to their inbred German speaking colony. The military and the police are distrusted and many crimes go unreported mainly due to a lack of faith in the police as capable or willing to do anything, particularly when there is no financial incentive involved. It is often possible to pay your way out of a crime and, in addition, jailbreaks are almost commonplace. It is a country with little preparation for tourism yet boasts some of the most remarkably preserved archaeological sites such as the ruins of the Jesuit missions.

That was the Arajua I knew and while many things have changed over the years, I fear too much has remained the same. The 21st century brought fancy shopping malls, an immense amount of cinemas weirdly enough, and an influx of development projects. But the truth is it's the same as surrounding a decaying body with sweet smelling flowers to hide the smell. Some things are rotten at the heart of the country. Then again if you look behind the façade aren't all countries the same? It's always easier to criticise looking outwards than to turn to what is on our own doorstep.

Arajuans themselves tend to drift along, notorious for their laid-back attitude and general apathy that affects all that they do. There is rarely any hurry or any planning, and retrospective memory is selective at best with little discussion or analysis of things past. Many Arajuans view themselves as victims of their indigenous heritage, a heritage that believes and teaches the value of living for the day, with no future projection or planning. There is no tomorrow and while this mentality has left Arajua backward in many aspects and riddled with political, economic and social problems, it appears to also have served as a mechanism for survival from the political oppression Arajuans have been subjected to for centuries.

During the time I spent in Arajua I learned to expect the unexpected. I learned the hard way that all my assumptions on people's behaviour were founded on a basis that did not exist in this land. So I should not have been surprised by what happened. Yet I was and very much so. Now I think perhaps I was more surprised at myself. Surprised that I accepted all that happened as if they were normal events and that I also became a willing participant in them.

I was driving with a friend to a meeting one afternoon – we were working on a joint project that had been riddled with problems and she, in her wisdom, had sought advice from a shaman to root out the source of our problems (as one does). This in itself in not uncommon in South America and so, while I inwardly scoffed, I nodded and accepted this approach without too much thought. But then she informed, as if it were the most normal thing in the world, that she had shown the shaman some photos and when he saw mine, he had jumped back with the shocked exclamation that an egun was surrounding my aura. A what? I had no idea what she was talking about. Moreover I was knocked off balance by her serious attitude in what she was sharing, a topic we had never discussed before and one in which I had no idea she was quite so involved. She explained that eguns are spirits that live among us from the ex-living, the energy that remains from the breath of life. "Ex-living" was her way of sugar-coating the word 'dead'. Most of us are blind to their existence, yet they see us and commune with us on a daily basis guiding us to better living or guiding us through difficult times. So far so good I thought. But of course there was to be a caveat. It all depended on what type of egun it was. And mine, as it turned out, was evil!

I am sometimes amazed by myself. When I tell this story people are often confused as to why I wasn't disturbed by either the mention of a shaman or the explanation of the egun, not to mention the fact that it was evil. I often fail to see the look of horror that comes across people's face when I mention the shaman, so they are still catching up with their horror when I hit them with the egun part, the evil egun part to be precise. Some start looking around nervously unsure of whether there are eguns hanging around I imagine (yes there are just in case you were wondering); others probably panicking that I am possessed and a horror movie is about to play out in front of their eyes. I'm never sure how to explain or justify my non-chalant telling of the story, but for the record I would like to acknowledge that I too am slightly disturbed by the fact that I wasn't more disturbed. Perhaps I was in shock at the time and not fully absorbing what I was hearing. In terms of my calm retelling of the story, well so much has happened since that these events seem neither odd nor rare anymore. Sometimes however I forget that is not the case for other people. I do try to reassure people that I have no evil spirits (that I know of) currently around me. Over time I also learned that some stories are not meant to be shared.

As time has passed, I have become even more complacent and unwavering as I come up against mysterious and strange things and I do wonder at times what this reveals about me. Without doubt my complacency often upsets people more than the actual events oddly enough. But telling the story of what was to happen next becomes so ridiculous that most people stop believing it could possibly be true before I have ever finished telling it. If I hadn't been there, with front row seats, I think I'd have a problem believing it too.

After a series of questions and answers the situation, in as much as it could be, was clarified. Simply put, someone had put a spell on me that consisted of an evil egun (in other words a nasty dead thing) surrounding and blocking my aura; this meant that no good could get out or in and I was destined to be plagued by bad luck and misfortune until such times as the egun was removed. Looking back I wondered if my life had been marked by any particular misfortune of late, bad luck was no rarity in my life and I did wonder for a while if the egun hadn't been some kind of evil gift at birth as opposed to a more recent spell! However I found it hard to imagine myself as a modern-day Sleeping Beauty, well at any rate I was quite sure my parents would have mentioned an evil witch bursting in on my Christening and cursing me. At this point I feel I should confess a series of strange things had been happening that I had put down to 'me being me', my general accident-prone nature. Things had happened that I had just accepted without question but the truth is they were far from regular.

Actually writing this I think it's even funnier that I didn't think anything was out of the ordinary, after all the previous month I had been involved in four road accidents; one each week and two of them on the same number of bus in exactly the same place. Every accident had also occurred on a Friday. What is wrong with me that I ever accepted this as normal? They had all been accidents that had brought about head injuries, something that became more pertinent as I delved more into this strange world. I don't know why this never occurred to me as odd. I think life in Arajua was so peculiar already that it failed to stand out. The first time I had been on the number 23 bus (you don't forget these details). I had fallen against a window on the bus as it crashed. My head slammed against the glass breaking it but leaving me with nothing more than a bruise on my forehead; the second accident had seen me thrown in a car and my head smash off the dashboard; in the third, once again on the number 23 bus, I was propelled from the back of the bus where I had been waiting to get off, to the front alongside the driver where I battered my head on the metal railings of the turnstile to board the bus; and the fourth, the worst and most bizarre, saw me hurled through the windscreen of a car but, as I managed somehow to hit the rear view mirror first, I went straight through the windscreen unbelievably without a scratch. I landed flat on the bonnet of the car and remember lying there listening to the shrieks of onlookers and the horrified scream of my friend who had been driving. As everyone rushed to the front of the car however they realised, somewhat disappointedly I might add, that I was miraculously unscathed and there was no blood to be seen. Naturally I did find it somewhat frustrating that these things were happening, but had slipped into a routine of expecting an accident to occur by the end of each week. It had simply become a part of my weekly routine.

On confiding in a friend who lived by the spiritual path of the native Arajuani Indians I was offered a new insight into these events. Her explanation was that the accidents would continue until I paid attention to what I was being taught and learned the lesson being offered me. This stems from the belief that all accidents and illnesses serve as a warning to us – a sudden jolt to pay attention to 'something' or 'someone'; apparently not even the common cold is simply caught, rather it is sent to us for a reason. I tried for endless periods of time to work out what I was being taught by these accidents but came up with very little other than the idea that perhaps I should walk more and stay away from cars and buses. And, of course, always to wear a seatbelt (not so straightforward in a country where many of the cars don't even have them). Although I laughed dismissively at her explanation, something about it made sense. Actually ten years before, a very similar thing happened and I kept having the most incredible accidents that involved, every time, an injury to my head. On one occasion I actually walked into a moving bus – an incredible feat by anyone's imagination. In any case the accidents stopped so I must have learned my lesson, although I remain ignorant to this day what these lessons actually were.

Returning to my egun. It appeared that I needed to go talk to a shaman who practised white magic about how to remove my evil companion. Apparently there are shaman of black or white magic and then there are those who dabble in both. Although surely if they are dabbling in any kind of black magic, they can't be all that good? Black magic definitely seemed something to stay well away from, although I must admit I wasn't convinced about seeing a shaman at all, black, white or any other shade for that matter! I felt I was committing some sinful deed that would bring the wrath of my childhood Catholic God upon me. Plus a part of me didn't really believe the whole thing and was finding the concept more and more ridiculous to accept. My strict Catholic upbringing and my Catholic guilt have been well ingrained into the very essence of my being. I kept imagining my involvement with the shaman would result in my condemnation to hell for all eternity. These days I realise everything that subsequently occurred is probably low down on the list of reasons why I may be succumbing to the fires of hell when I die. The less said about that the better. Despite all the doubts I had, not to mention that little voice in the back of my head telling me I could be losing my mind, I went for a long drive with my friend one Sunday morning to a house in the countryside (in the middle of nowhere) where my ordeal was to begin. Some might say that I was tempting fate by delving further into the issue. In retrospect I'd probably have to agree, though that would not change the choices I made. My life has never been the same since the series of events set in motion that day.

"How dramatic mi hija." Andres was shaking with *laughter.*

42

"What? I'm telling it as it was."

"If you say so." Andres' laughter continued.

"Trust me I don't need to add any creative touches to what happened...to what you put me through." But Andres had stopped listening. "The truth is bad enough!" Andres stopped laughing long enough to drink some water, but before I could speak the laughter had returned.

"Stop mi hija. It really is too much."

The house was typical of the area: roughly built and unfinished, a malnourished looking dog tied to a post which barely raised its head as we passed, chickens running aimlessly around a garden which was a mixture of red earth and sand, the kind that always stained your socks and the bottom of your trousers. An ancient toothless woman was sitting on a rocking chair in the shade, nodding and laughing as we approached making me feel distinctly uneasy as if she knew something that I did not. As she smiled the wrinkles moved around her face showing areas of deep-set tan in a rippling effect as one line rolled upon another meeting in a cluster at the base of her neck. Some children, clad in a variety of mis-fitting and faded football shirts were playing in the yard, regularly upsetting the occasional tranquillity of the chickens. They stopped and looked at us nodding in recognition at my friend and giggling almost uncontrollably at me. Oh my God! Could they all see my egun? I began to feel as if I were the devil himself, evil incarnate come to beg for redemption. I felt incredibly guilty even though I had done no wrong, at least that I was aware of. Guilty for having somehow managed to attain an egun and guilty to my western Catholic upbringing which I was certain would well and truly scold me for the course of action I was about to take. Scold me? Excommunicate me more like!

I entered the house hesitantly, with a sinking feeling that this had not been such a good idea after all. Suddenly I was feeling confident that I could just learn to live with my egun. How hard could it be? I mean I hadn't even known it was there before so we were obviously getting along relatively well!

The house was even less constructed on the inside than on the outside. Homes in the Arajuan countryside have a tendency to be built piecemeal, as and when the occupants have the money to do so. However they rarely wait until they have the money to complete the job before they move in, merely adding to parts as and when finances allow and, in the end, it resembles a roughly constructed jigsaw formed from a variety of pieces that never quite fit. From the lack of construction I couldn't help but doubt how successful this shaman actually was. If he were good at his job wouldn't he be a wealthy man with an expensive house? Then again if he were wealthy it would probably mean he was taking advantage of poor cursed souls like me.

A kitchen area was marked out by imaginary walls – construction had begun and been abandoned a long time ago, the living area was practically bare. It stretched over almost the whole ground floor which was earthen in some areas and in the process of being tiled in others (a process that also appeared to have been abandoned). In the left-hand corner was a table and two chairs, behind this table a door. The table itself was covered with various artefacts, small statues, stones, plants, sticks and cut up pieces of paper at one end and small plates with various pulses, wheat and spices and little bowls of water at the other. There was a build-up of dust resting on any free space in the room. Two boys who looked to be in their early teens stood in the kitchen area talking to each other in Arajuani; the indigenous language I was unfamiliar with at that time, except for some of the rudest expressions I have ever known in my life. For reasons I cannot quite explain they are also expressions I have a tendency to use on a regular basis. I think it's a foreign language thing whereby cursing never sounds so bad when it's not in your native language. Before you know it, you've developed a form of Tourette's Syndrome that you not only consider acceptable, but also think it makes you sound exotic!

Standing around waiting, without knowing what I was actually waiting for, my glance turned towards the upstairs area from which a strange noise was coming. A small winding stairway with no banister circled the area above the table. Wires stuck out of the concrete in various unfinished areas and I noticed the floor actually stopped short of a final door which, I later learned, led to the bathroom. There were three other doors all, I presumed, leading to bedrooms. The house was large albeit incomplete.

After about fifteen minutes of painful waiting, a man I quickly learned to be a shaman by the name of Andres, came out from one of the upstairs rooms. My friend met him with an embrace and they muttered some words ensuring I could not hear, before she turned to me saying, "There is nothing more I can do, I've brought you here, you're in his hands now. I must wait outside. He has to see if he can help you first." And with that she left, abandoning me to my fate.

"What?!" I called after her, my voice breaking from a mix of shock and fear. It came out as both a question and an exclamation of horror. This was news to me. I thought I was here to be helped and had no idea there was still some kind of initiation process I had to go through to be approved. Wasn't it enough that I had actually turned up? I needed references too? From dead people? Seriously? The shaman took a seat at the table and signalled for me to do the same. Part of me believed – wanted to believe - that at any minute my friends would jump out laughing at my stupidity for being in this ridiculous situation. I desperately wanted to believe that it was all an elaborate joke and I was secretly being filmed for some hilarious 'caught on camera television show. Although how I would ever explain allowing myself to be in that situation in the first place I don't know. Another part of me feared the unknown of what could possibly be about to happen next.

The shaman was a man in his late forties or early fifties. It was hard to tell and there was a certain youthfulness in his face despite the wrinkles. His long grey hair was tied back in a ponytail that had to be draped over his shoulder as he sat to avoid him sitting on it. His skin was a deep sallow colour and his face appeared soft and gentle until he smiled and betrayed a bottom row of yellow rotting teeth that gave his appearance a hint of maliciousness.

"This is too much!" laughed Andres.

"I told you – that's how I remember it." I replied defensively. "Admittedly the teeth have improved – you must have had some work done. You must be earning more these days." We both laughed.

"Your imagination has no bounds. You should write a book about it all one day you know."

"I might just do that Andres. I might just do that."

He was dressed in white cotton clothing and wore a pair of flip-flops. The most striking and unnerving aspect of his appearance however were his nails. They were so long that they had begun to curl and turn yellowish at the ends. And as he sat at the table with his hands lying atop it was as if he was pulling me in as he constantly moved his figures around, his nails winding hypnotically in front of me. Perhaps this was the moment I should have run and never looked back, but something made me stay, something more than curiosity. In a strange way none of this seemed new. A part of me was terrified but another part was curious and excited. The truth is I wanted to be there. I felt I was exactly where I was supposed to be.

He sat staring at me for a while, grinning occasionally and unsettling me with the occasional flash of his teeth.

Apparently, as I later learned, he was learning about my egun, and the trapped aura underneath it, as he studied me. He then explained that he would have to ask 'the gods' if any were prepared to help me. Gods? Plural? How many are there? Without their support he was unable to agree to help me, as their rejection would signify my evil nature's predominance. He told me that morning a man had come to him for help but all the spirits and gods had denied him so he had immediately, and quite literally, chased him away and immediately cleansed the room and the air of the evil he had brought with him. Now I was getting worried. Don't get me wrong, I'm not evil but I'm no saint either and I wasn't too sure where the bar for the shaman's standards was being set. Suddenly he proceeded to whisper to some shells and wave his hands around, rolling his eyes to the back of his head from time to time. I'm sure he did this for my benefit to add some dramatic effect. Then he shook another pile of shells in his hands. Finally he threw them onto the table between some beads, sticks and stones. Slowly he began to extract some and then stopped to 'read' the message left on the table. He then shared the good news – apparently *all* the gods had come to my aid without exception and on his first request. I must admit that my relief at this news was only slightly superseded by a shameful notion of pride in what I took to imply my inherent goodness. I had passed the first test and, it would appear, with flying colours. Here's hoping the rest would be that simple I thought misguidedly.

Andres stood up and walked around to the back of my chair, pointlessly telling me not to be concerned, and began to hover his hands around the crown of my head and chant. Then he stepped to the side with a look of weariness and one of the teenage boys, whose presence I had completely forgotten about, came rushing up with a glass of water and a small towel. Andres sat down and raised his hand to silence the questions that I was clearly about to ask. So many things were racing around my head and my mouth was opened slightly as I had been about to begin a torrent of questions. My discomfort was increasing rapidly and the more nervous I became, the more difficult it seemed to string together a sentence in Spanish and the few times I did manage to speak I stuttered and confused my words.

Andres finally spoke, "You should know that your head is open."

I looked at him more than a little bemused.

"You have a hole in your head!" he added as if this suddenly made his statement clearer and more logical. I continued to stare back in confusion, resisting the urge to check that the top of my head was still intact and decisively closing my mouth just in case that was the opening he was referring to. "That is why the spirits are drawn to you. And it is why you are susceptible to the darkness of others – to their spells."

"Spells!" I shrieked, "Plural!" How many eguns could one person have? I began to panic as I made a mental not to myself to read up on this stuff.

"You must learn to use this gift, to train yourself," he said decisively, "or we must close your head for good…for your own protection."

Without hesitation I replied in an abnormally loud voice and without any consideration for what it might entail or what any of it even meant, "Close it!"

Dismissively Andres explained that he would have to consult the spirits on the process to remove my egun and when that was complete, he would close my head. My head could not possibly be closed apparently until the egun was gone.

During the next hour consults were made with invisible 'forces' to decide the course of action to remove my egun. The removal itself would be carried out in the course of a day, but there were follow up steps (of course there would be) to prevent a return and secure my future safety and protection. It was all to begin the next week with a trip to a place of 'fresh falling water'. In Arajua, the landlocked, very flat, sun baked hub of Latin America, finding fresh falling water is a mission in itself, in some areas simply finding water is no easy task. Of course it transpired there was a waterfall in a national park a mere 400km away. It was decided that the trip would take place on the Wednesday of that week. We would leave at 6am and Andres would bring the necessary provisions. My only instructions were to come dressed completely in white.

On the Wednesday morning I arrived punctually as arranged. Clad in white from head to foot I resembled a fat, misguided fairy that had just fallen from the top of a Christmas tree – I defy anybody to look good dressed top to toe in white unless they are a catwalk model. I had told nobody where I was going and had made up a story, avoiding the truth at any cost. How could I possibly begin to explain what was happening or, more to the point, why I was agreeing to be involved in it? The journey and the not knowing what lay ahead, increased the anxious hours of an already lengthy trip. Nobody spoke (at least not to me or in a language I could understand). It was as if I didn't exist and each time I tried to discover what to expect, I was quickly silenced and told not to worry, that I would discover soon enough. But I *was* worried.

You see there is one thing I have omitted to explain. On the Sunday as my shaman had listed all he would need for the various ceremonies, I was sure I had heard him mention something about needing to use chickens. From that day I had been having visions of exsanguinated or decapitated chickens being placed before me as I was forced to drink cups of their blood or being ordered to bite the head off a live chicken. And I was terrified…not least because I am a vegetarian.

Eventually we arrived, parked the car, gathered up a variety of bags, and began walking through the trees that led to the waterfall. It has crossed my mind that I didn't know these people, that they could be taking me to this remote place and using me as a sacrificial offering and no one would ever know. I would simply disappear. They might even belong to a cult group of serial killers. If someone else told me this story I would think that they were mad for taking part in it all so naively. I would have found their involvement in such activities incomprehensible. It's like those horror movies where you sit shouting at the screen about how stupid the people are for not seeing that something bad was *obviously* going to happen to them. Yet although I questioned what was happening, although I was afraid, I couldn't shake the feeling that it was something I simply *had* to do. It never once occurred to me not to keep going with it all. Maybe I was just too far into it at that stage. While there was a fear, it was a strange kind of fear, predominated by a sense of excitement.

We reached a clearing in the trees and stopped. The waterfall, though still not in sight, could be heard in the near distance. The shaman spoke to the others and they all began unpacking various bags and then promptly disappeared. I was told to stand in a certain place where there was a clearing among the trees and four candles were placed around me marking the points of the compass. Then he opened the various bags which appeared to be wheat, flour and various other powdery food substances. After strictly and repeatedly (and unnecessarily in my opinion) instructing me to be silent, he said a prayer in which he called on the gods to hold firm in their promise of help as we approached this testing moment. That's what he told me anyway, the truth is I didn't understand a word of it and for all I knew he could have been calling the prince of darkness to come and take me to be his bride. I'm a trusting soul all of a sudden at the oddest of times! Then he lifted a handful of each substance and dropped it on my head!

Wheat, flour and much more were systematically poured over the top of my head where it began to form a small mountain, while other parts sprinkled over my clothes, my eyelashes, some had managed to find its way into my eyes and mouth, not to mention up my nose. As if all of that wasn't bad enough, he then proceeded to rub it into the top of my head! I consoled myself with the thought that it might act as a good hair conditioner. Bewildered as I was, I stood firm, still trying ever so hard to keep my mouth tightly closed, not one of my strong points. Then Andres took out some eggs and told me that he would place them at various joints of my body and I had to stand for a period of time holding these eggs. He then added that if they broke, it was a sign of the evil in me resisting his help. This seemed a little unfair, after all I had the ingredients for a cake balanced on my head, a strange man chanting unintelligible words and encircling me continuously, and now I had to attempt a circus act with some eggs! In the fairy stories I read as a child breaking spells was a hell of a lot easier – go to sleep for a hundred years, kiss a toad, have a prince turn up and kiss me. No such luck for me. I got to dress like the Michelin Man, be covered in foodstuffs (which incidentally were starting to leave unsightly stains on my beautiful white clothes) and now do a trick with some eggs! Andres placed an egg in each elbow and under my armpits, one between my knees, thighs and ankles and finally one under my chin – something which entailed the lowering of my head and with it, the collapse of the powdery stuff from my head down my face. He stood back, lit the candles and instructed me to pray. And I did! I prayed like never before, but I doubt it was for any of the things he intended.

After an interminable period he stepped into the circle and removed the eggs I had been balancing around the joints of my body for what seemed like an eternity. Then, after all my painful agility in this task, Andres smashed them at my feet and poured wax from the candles over the mixture. Still quite shocked and tense from the strain of trying not to drop the eggs, I wearily, or rather warily, awaited my next instructions. After blowing out the candles and covering everything with earth, the shaman instructed me to follow him through the trees to the waterfall. He strode off leaving me to run behind, trying to catch up as I left a trail of cake mixture with every step. At least I thought, it would be easy to find my way back.

On reaching the water's edge Andres jumped expertly from various stones to reach a large plateau like area where he sat down and crossed his legs. I however was told to walk into the water. Now, two things were troubling me at this point. "Only two?" I hear you ask! First, I hadn't failed to notice numerous signs warning people to stay out of the water due to sudden plunging depths and the general danger of the surrounding area. Second, the water was freezing beyond belief and the idea of submerging myself in this ice-cold water, particularly fully clad, was a little disconcerting. Added to that of course is the fact that my swimming skills at that time were weak at best and I have a terror of being in any water where I cannot firmly place my feet on the ground, see them, and have my head fully above the water all at the same time. Did I say only two things were troubling me? I lied. On a positive note, the whole experience did spur me on to take swimming lessons, just in case I should be required to plunge into any watery depths to remove any future eguns. I like to be prepared.

I took my first trembling steps into the water, gasping at the coldness. In a country as hot as Arajua, it seemed unimaginable that the water could possibly be so cold ... but it was. When it reached waist level, something which took forever as I was terrified with every step I took feeling for secure ground before I dared move forward another step, Andres told me to stop. He closed his eyes and begin to pray, oblivious to how cold and terrified I was. I had no idea what I was supposed to do and as he prayed, I found my mind distracted by thoughts of drowning or simply dying of hypothermia. But I had come this far, there was no point in turning back now I told myself. He proceeded to tie a slim rope around the top of each of his arms, explaining that they were a method of protection from evil and that, in time, I would receive my own. Lucky me! Each rope was hand woven according to the needs of the owner he told me. While obviously I looked forward to receiving my protective ropes one day, the cold and my general discomfort were a test of my interest in such details at this point.

Andres told me that as I submerged myself completely (what?) under the water for a period of time (you've got to be kidding), my egun would attack him in an attempt to stay with me and resist his powers. Nobody had told me these details beforehand and, if they had, it is highly unlikely I would have embarked on this journey. In fact there had been a significant and constant failure to communicate or explain anything. He told me not to be disturbed by what I saw. (Erm no!) I looked at him more than a little doubtful that anything was capable of seriously disturbing me more than I already had been. I fixed him with an angry stare as I tried to convey the certainty that I was not about to submerge myself under this water for any period of time be it short or long!

Needless to say I did indeed submerge myself, and repeatedly as it turned out. Apparently I never stayed under long enough and so Andres constantly, and very unsympathetically I might add, shouted at me to go under again and again and each time for longer. Some time later when our friendship had developed and I had come to trust Andres, he told me I was more testing than the egun itself, that he'd never known anyone to talk and complain so much during one of these ceremonies. He commented that it would all have gone more smoothly if they had tied me down and gagged me. To this day I don't know if he was joking. After my lengthiest submersion he began to cry in a most animated fashion that my egun had detached itself from me and pointed to an area of water that was beginning to flow downstream. Immediately I looked to where he was pointing, curious and excited to see what my departing egun looked like. But all I could see was a circle of grease from all the stuff that I had been covered in earlier, floating away, albeit reluctantly, from my side. Who knew that a departing egun looks like a pool of grease? But who am I to question the mystical ways?

"You are so disrespectful at times." Commented Andres, shaking his head in mock despair.

"Where's your sense of humour?"

"Where was yours?" Andres fired back.

"Are you honestly telling me that my evil egun took the form of a pool of grease?" I asked laughing.

"Making jokes to avoid yet again mi hija?"

"And what is it you think I'm avoiding?"

"Ah mi hija where do I begin? Life. Living. Accepting." Andres paused, "Forgiving..."

Cutting him off I shouted, "Forgiving? Forgiving? Who the hell am I supposed to be forgiving?" I couldn't even explain why that word had made me feel so angry all of a sudden. "Tell me!"

"Yourself."

Groaning I replied, "I hate it when you say things like that."

"Because I'm right?"

"No! Because it's irritating and unhelpful. Just like you!"

"A rather fitting description of yourself I think." The grinning Andres replied.

It was at this point however that the shaman began to shake violently. While part of me (most of me) dismissed this as a theatrical show to convert my doubting mind, the convulsions continued beyond what seemed permissible for a joke. I was becoming more and more uncomfortable as Andres' fit appeared to become less and less controllable. Panic was setting in that he would fall off his precipice or start choking on his tongue. I was also acutely aware that I was too far away to do anything and my poor swimming skills ensured I'd never reach him on time. I stood there, waist high in the freezing water, helpless and paralysed as I watched him. And then something strange occurred for which, no matter how I search, I can offer no explanation. I had clearly watched the shaman knot the ropes tightly around the tops of his arms yet, as he tossed his head in what I later learned was a struggle with the newly released egun, I saw the ropes untie themselves and slide down his arms to his wrists. No doubt there are many logical explanations for this, I could probably think of a few myself, but seeing it happen refuted the logic that would try to explain it. I swear I saw those ropes literally untie themselves from the knots that Andres had formed as if invisible hands were manipulating them. And then, as quickly as they had begun, the convulsions stopped. Andre sat there, slumped over and clearly exhausted, but alive. I began to speak but he immediately raised his hand to silence me. His hand hovered there in the air ensuring he made his point clearly that he wanted silence.

Confused, cold and somewhat shrivelled up, I was eventually allowed to leave the water. I no longer felt the icy cold of the water, or most of my limbs for that matter. What I felt most of all for some reason was an overwhelming sense of self-pity. My egun had departed (so Andres assured me) and I was cleansed. Andres informed me that under no circumstances should I dry myself, but to let the sun embrace me. He then pointed to an area far from the others, telling me to go sit alone and contemplate 'my path'. Meanwhile he joined the others and, seated in comfort, they all ate a hearty lunch. It would appear that my personal spiritual path did not include food!

"Change happens incrementally mi hija. You want everything now."

"I just want to understand."

"I want! I want! I want! Let go of your ego." Andres waved his hand dismissively as he spoke. His words made me sound so selfish and I could feel my face burn with shame and anger.

"It's easy for you Andres. You sit there with your riddles and explanations that nobody else can understand. You chose this path. I didn't. I don't want it."

"You cannot change what is and complaining about it will not help. Create your own opportunities instead of complaining." He replied warily.

"What do you want me to do. Leap into all of this as if it's normal?"

"Leap, no. Lean, yes. Create your own opportunities. Don't wait for others to do it for you." Andres paused as if he planned to say more, but instead he stood up and walked to the door. At the door he paused once more and then, without turning to look at me, commented loudly. "You can't plant an apple seed and expect a banana to grow."

Inside my head I was screaming.

My clothes dried quickly in the scorching heat of the afternoon sun, as I sat thinking about everything that had happened. Looking at it from the outside I could see how entertaining it all was and I could laugh at the role I was unwittingly yet somehow willingly playing. But another part of me felt a growing restlessness as if something, I couldn't quite grasp what, was coming, something big. I couldn't help but feel both fearful and apprehensive. Whatever was coming, be it good or bad, I knew for sure it would be life changing. My thoughts were interrupted as the group started to pack up. As the sun began to set, we headed off on the long drive home.

The trip home was once again in silence, only this time I was glad of it. The myriad of questions had condensed into emptiness. I no longer sought explanations of events passed or yet to come. As they dropped me off, Andres explained that the next part of the process would involve me bathing in specially prepared herbs at the same time daily for seven days. Great! The first day however, he explained, would require an initiation ceremony first so would take longer. How many initiation hurdles was I going to have to jump before this was over, I wondered. He told me to come to his home at midday the next day to begin this. Nobody ever asked if I was free and available to meet these requests. There was a clear assumption that I was and if not, that I would cancel any and every other plan. And I always did. With an inward groan and a growing sense of dismay that all of this might go on endlessly, I agreed. I couldn't help but wonder yet again why the removal of evil spells could not be just a little more straightforward.

The next day I arrived punctually once again and entered the shaman's home after passing the old woman, the children and the crazy chickens all of whom seemed to be fixtures of the garden. Did these children never go to school? Did they leave grandma in the garden indefinitely? Why did she laugh every time she saw me? Were those the chickens he used for …. Oh no! I had to get those thoughts out of my mind and fast.

On entering the house I saw that the floor had been marked out in parts with a white powder. The shapes seemed suspiciously evil to me as one most definitely looked like a trident – the kind you see Satan carrying in pictures! I was hustled into the middle of a large circle and told to straddle the fork like shape. And, once again, I obliged pushing all my fears and concerns to the back of my mind. Honestly, I'm not sure I did push them to the back of my mind, I just agreed to do what they asked of me every time, no matter how odd or suspicious it seemed; no matter what that little voice in my head tried to scream in warning. What is wrong with me? Candles were lit and chanting began. The two teenage boys were now active participants and the whole thing was starting to take on darker connotations as it progressed. I certainly no longer expected to discover I was the butt of a hilarious joke. My eyes were firmly fixed on the door as I planned how I would quickly run out, grabbing my bag and car keys, jump into my car and drive away never to return. I planned and planned my escape while my feet remained firmly on the ground. I was going nowhere and I knew it.

At one point Andres ceased chanting briefly to tell me that in what would now follow, whatever I did, I was never to look down. He then continued as before. Now seriously? Somebody tells you whatever you do you must not look down – what would you do? I mean as an avid bible reader – well a forced bible reader at any rate – the story of Lot's wife should be a warning to all to obey instruction. However Lot's wife shows us that transitioning from one level to another is rarely smooth and change is often fraught with trials, as I was about to find out. The man never explained anything or warned me before, so inevitably my curiosity was piqued. Naturally I was overcome with the urge to look down, partly I admit from fear of someone crawling between my straddling legs. Curiosity, fear – whatever, it's human nature. So of course I looked down and as I did, I rapidly discovered that the warning was a very practical instruction and nothing else. But it was too late. The white powder which, of course, turned out to be gun powder, had been set alight. As it spread through all the connecting points it fired between my legs into a small but significant explosion. As I looked down this blast sparked towards my face catching the side of my long flowing hair (would it have been too much trouble for them to suggest I tie it back?) which began to smoulder slightly. I, and I alone, panicked. Andres stopped briefly, irritated by my 'stupidity' and handed me a wet cloth. The fact that he had the cloth ready surely implied he had seen that coming and I had a bad feeling that they were all enjoying this just a little too much. After reiterating how foolish I was and telling me at unnecessary length about how I never listen, the chanting continued. Everyone seemed oblivious to my horror and discomfort, and as I looked sideways I couldn't help but notice that the right side of my once long flowing locks was decidedly shorter than the other.

When this ceremony was complete, I was told that a bucket of herbs was awaiting me in the bathroom and that I should wash myself with them for ten minutes exactly. I climbed the unfinished stairs remembering that the floor was incomplete and stopped short of the door. I stretched across and pushed the door open before jumping across the abyss! A large bucket full of dried herbs of assorted smells (none of them pleasant) was awaiting me and so, resigned to my fate, I undressed. Cautiously I turned on the shower, which only offered freezing cold water, and began to rub the foul smelling mix all over my body. There was no towel to dry myself as I had been told I must allow my body to dry naturally. As I dressed my dampened clothes soaked in the aroma of the foul smelling herbs. I drove all the way back with the windows down hoping this would help alleviate the odour before I returned to work, but it did little to help. I returned to work reeking of the malodorous concoction. Andres had informed me that I could not wash again for eight hours or the herbs would not work their magic.

I sat in work trying to look nonchalant as people around remarked on the strange, somewhat vile stench in the area. I joined in, asking what it could possibly be and where it might be coming from. My colleagues came to the conclusion that the drains must be blocked and the smell was coming from the toilet. I nodded in agreement at which point one side of my once long hair with its burnt ends, fell across my face. I quickly tucked it behind my ear and made a mental note to cut the other side at home to even it out. I had told my work, in the most incredible lie, that I had to receive physiotherapy for a knee problem for eight days at exactly the same time every day. They said nothing, not even when I returned smelling oddly every day, nor did anybody comment on my new bizarre hairdo. And so for the next few days I lied to my employer in order to leave work for my midday bathing.

I would arrive each day at the home of the shaman and, after the first day, my presence was rarely acknowledged. I would climb the stairs and take my leap of faith over into the bathroom where the bucket of herbs awaited me. Some days I considered only pretending to wash, put off by the lingering smell, the freezing water and how ridiculous the whole thing seemed. But then I thought if my egun found its way back to me he would know I hadn't done what I was supposed to. Then I would be in so much more trouble…as if that were possible.

Throughout this week of repeated bathing, I still had at the back of my mind the unanswered question regarding the chickens. Various times I had tried to get more information but never very successfully. Andres generally ignored me altogether, and his young helpers simply burst into fits of laughter each time I came near, and since the egun was now apparently gone, I could only assume that this was now personal. At this stage my fear of being made bite the heads off chickens, or some such similar behaviour was causing me many a restless night. As my seven days bathing drew to a close, I was given a day and time to appear for the final ceremony. At this point I could hold back no longer.

"I will not drink chicken blood!" I blurted out all of a sudden, I'd like to think with measured hysteria. "Nor will I bite heads off chickens." Andres stared back at me and I wasn't quite sure if he was surprised by my passionate outburst or amused. "You can't make me!" I continued while Andres sat back in his chair, arms folded, staring at me. Still he said nothing and I felt obliged to continue although I had no idea what else to say. "I'm telling you, you can't make me!" Andres continued to stare at me in silence. "I'm a vegetarian." I added meekly at which point Andres began howling with laughter, his two companions joining in.

"And why would I make you drink chicken blood and bite the heads off these poor animals?" Andres asked when he finally calmed down. I had no idea how to answer that.

"Isn't that what you people do?"

"And where did you get that idea?"

"Well..." that was a good question, "...television I guess." I was beginning to wish I had kept my mouth shut as the three of them erupted into laughter again.

"It is not our normal practice," began Andres, "but we could make an exception for you." Embarrassed but relieved I took that to mean exsanguinated chickens were not on the menu.

"Measured hysteria? That's not how I remember it!" Andres chuckled.

"You all got to have a laugh at my expense. Various times at that."

"No mi hija, we were just playing a little."

"Same thing."

"No, play is harmless and it is also necessary. We forget too quickly how to play like a child. Always in a hurry to grow up. That was you. Always in a hurry to finish and move on to the next thing."

"Did I forget to stop and smell the herbs?" I asked sarcastically.

"No. You forgot to breathe." Andres stared at me as he replied and I felt as if he were boring straight through to

my soul. Something about the way he looked made me think the comment was not what it seemed on the surface. I looked back unsure what to say.

"I'm tired Andres. Tired of thinking..."

"Overthinking."

"I don't know how to stop."

"You think about everything to avoid thinking about something." Andres chuckled to himself, "focus on the something."

"What's that supposed to mean? Oh don't tell me I have to work it out for myself, or I will learn with time, or some other crap!" Andres lifted his eyes and gave me one of his weary looks I had seen way too often. "No profound comment then?" I offered sarcastically.

'Your anger exhausts me. What must it be doing to you?"

"I'm not angry!"

Andres smiled and spoke with a softened voice, "What are you then?"

"Lost."

V

The day of the final ceremony approached and oh how I looked forward to my return to normality. How naïve could I have been! Little did I realise then that there would be no normality to return to; that the normality I thought I had been living was simply an elaborate illusion.

"You were always in such a rush to get to the end, reach your destination."

"What's wrong with that?"

"It is the journey that is so important not the destination. Haven't you learned that? As we walk upon this earth our feet press against the bones of the ancestors on whose shoulders we stand. Every step should be taken with care and respect."

"So what happens when I reach my destination? Enlightenment? Peace? Happiness?"

Andres roared with laughter, "Mi hija don't you see? When you reach your destination the journey begins all over again."

"You're not selling it very well you know?" I replied horrified by the concept of my never-ending journey. But Andres was no longer listening to me as he continued to laugh as if he'd heard the funniest joke ever told. Well maybe he had and it was called 'my life'!

"The journey is a chance to learn the stories of those who came before us. To know the stories of your ancestors is to know your own story and to know your own story is to truly understand where you are from. When you know where you are from, mi hija, you will know where you are going. And then, when you finally know where you are going you will know how to dream outside of the box that

63

*so many have, and will continue to try to put you in. To
dream outside of that man-made box is to know and believe
in all the possibilities in front of you."*

Once again the floor had been marked out with white
powder, resulting in me immediately tying my hair back
securely. At least I was learning. I couldn't help but notice
there was a small cage like box in the corner, housing four
rather noisy chickens. What if they had lied to me, mocking
my fear of biting the heads off chickens? It had been a ruse
to get me to this point and now what? Thoughts were racing
through my head as I imagined myself biting heads off
chickens and drinking their blood (I have no idea why my
imagination had me biting their heads off as opposed to a
handy machete being used for this purpose); or perhaps I
was the one to be sacrificed today, my life given up to the
'gods' as an offering now that I had been cleansed of my
evil egun... Rather disturbingly, drinking the chicken blood
seemed to upset me more than being killed as a sacrifice!

Before my thoughts could wander any further, I was
ushered into the middle of the circle, candles were lit and
the chanting began. I stood to the best of my attention but
the sight of the chickens had returned all my primal fears
and I couldn't help myself from giggling occasionally and
somewhat uncontrollably. You see I have two defaults
when under stress or feeling attacked. The first and most
used by far, is that I resort to sarcasm although I prefer to
call it wit, but due to the opinions of others that is up for
debate. The second, when I cannot speak for whatever
reason, and that is a rare occurrence I'm told, I start to
giggle.

In this instance my laughter was most definitely a
nervous reaction as I had long since failed to find any
amusement in these events – although I have since
developed a very dark humour based on my 'black magic'
experiences. Each time I giggled I was severely scolded by

Andres. One of the most laid-back individuals I have ever met was beginning to crack under the pressure of working with me! Suddenly he stopped and with a controlled but raised voice informed me that my lack of concentration and inability to appreciate the gravity of the matter meant we would have to start that section once again, adding that if my disrespectful behaviour continued we may have to repeat the entire process from day one. What? Say no more, there was absolutely no way I was going through all of that again and with that I stifled my nervous giggles as much as I possibly could.

"Would you really have made me do it all again?"

"It wasn't necessary. But you were being very annoying."

"But you said..."

"You behaved after that didn't you?" Andres interrupted chuckling, *"Well for the most part."*

"You lied to me!" I was more shocked by the fact that Andres had lied, that he could lie, than by the lie itself.

"No, I did not. Truth is malleable. You know that better than anyone." He gave me that look and I immediately turned my eyes away. I felt ashamed, discovered somehow, but I didn't even know why.

After what I am sure was an unnecessarily long chanting period, the shaman made his way to the chickens and extracted his first unwilling victim. He walked towards me chanting holding the chicken upside down by its feet. Apparently this prevents it from flapping around. Who knew? I have learned much of the habits of a chicken since that day or so I thought. On telling this story to a veterinary friend, I tried to impress her with my knowledge of chickens. She looked at me in disgust and explained that holding a chicken upside down has nothing to do with the flapping wings. She explained, in great detail, that as chickens have no diaphragm, holding them upside down limits their ability to breathe as their abdominal organs compress their air sacs. In other words, the chicken stopped flapping its wings because it was struggling to breathe and potentially dying...according to her... Personally I prefer my explanation, however I do feel obliged to share the official one in the interest of animal welfare and accompany it with the caveat that you should not try this at home. Come to think of it, I am slightly perturbed that my veterinary friend took the moral high ground over the issue of the flapping chicken wings (or lack of), as opposed to what happened next! I can assure you all I have never come into such close proximity with any since.

Gently swaying the chicken to and fro, the shaman stood before me, his eyes closed as he hummed a steady chant. The laughing boys who were on the outer edges of the circle, were kneeling and chanting in what appeared to be a response to Andres' words. I was now sweating profusely, terrified of what was about to happen. At that moment Andres opened his eyes, swinging the chicken even more violently than before, until it came full circle and ... he hit me on the head with it. Whatever horror I had been trying to prepare myself for, being bitch slapped by a chicken had not been on the list. I'm not joking, he whacked me on the top of my head and forcefully with a live, though somewhat stunned, chicken. Well the chicken wasn't the only one stunned I can assure you. I'm not sure who was more shocked, bruised or indignant about this event, but before either the chicken or I had time to recover, I found myself being slapped from head to foot, left to right by the swaying chicken in the hands of the over enthusiastic shaman. The poor chicken had become extremely vociferous about these activities, while I on the other hand had been rendered utterly speechless.

Eventually the beating concluded and the shaman returned the chicken to its cage to both of our relief. But as he turned around I saw that he had extracted another and was moving towards me with slight swaying movements. And so it was that I came to be beaten up by four chickens one sunny Sunday morning.

As it turned out the final chicken was actually a rooster (they all look the same to me, especially under duress) and after its involuntary slapping attack on me, I was told that he (the rooster) and I needed to talk! I was to tell the rooster all of my hopes and dreams for the future, as well as my fears. Andres held the rooster by the back of its neck and positioned him so that his 'beak' was almost touching my lips. From that position he told me I had to begin my conversation. As I tried to back away, Andres took me by the back of my neck with his free hand and brought us closer together again with considerable force. I was overwhelmed by the smell – it had never occurred to me that a chicken's breath could smell quite so bad, basically like rotting chicken!

Strangely the thought that popped into my head at this point was whether I should talk to the rooster in Spanish or English. I say strange because I think most 'normal' people would be wondering about so many other aspects of the situation. Anyway I decided to ask Andres what language to converse with the rooster in. He looked at me with a mixture of weariness and frustration, something I couldn't help but find a little ironic, if not downright unfair.

"The chickens understand all languages." Who knew poultry were such accomplished linguists?

Based on his reaction, apparently this was an obvious fact I should have somehow known. I'm unsure when Andres thought I'd been running around chatting to chickens in the past to have known this. My annoyance was curbed as I became acutely aware of the expectant faces around me so I decided the rooster and I had better start talking. After careful consideration, I opted for English as it made me feel slightly less ridiculous. I began in a clear loud voice, albeit somewhat self-consciously – after all I had never been quite so intimate with poultry before - only to be immediately silenced by a loud shushing noise and looks of horror all around me.

"You must whisper to the chicken – this information is private. Treat it with respect." Andres hissed at me in disgust.

Yet another *obvious* fact that must have escaped me. And if it was so private, why were they all standing there watching and listening to me? Anyway I began to whisper to the expectant rooster that day. I told the most unbelievable rubbish to a chicken that squawked continuously spraying me with gungy spit as it polluted my nasal cavities.

"It was definitely entertaining."

"Little did I know that, like the chicken, it seems you Andres understand all languages!"

Andres roared with laughter. "Not all. But I did enjoy your conversation."

"You shouldn't have been listening. Doesn't it say that somewhere in one of your shamanic rule books?"

"You shouldn't have spoken so loudly." Andres was still laughing as he remembered that fateful day, "And there's no rule book."

"So you make it up as you go along? I knew it."

"Perhaps. Why did you speak so loudly?"

"You didn't tell me not to." I paused, "Okay, the truth is ... I didn't know where his ear was." It was an honest and innocent statement. I'd never given it much thought before but I remember wondering that day and not daring to ask where a chicken's ears are. I still don't know. I mean, do they even have ears? My comment however had reduced Andres to a coughing fit from his hysterical laughter. "I hope you choke!" I replied indignantly.

"Really?"

"No… Well maybe just a little bit." We both looked at one another and laughed. *I never could stay angry at Andres, no matter how much he infuriated me with his riddles and tests.*

The conversation with the chicken unsurprisingly, if I am being honest, did not exactly flow. I had no idea what to say to him. Every time I thought I had said enough and could safely finish, the others continued to look expectantly and I knew I had to keep going. Trust me, the things I shared with that chicken no one would ever believe! At the end I was becoming 'giggly' again, much to Andres' annoyance until he could hold back no longer and blurted out, "Maya you do not appreciate how fortunate you have been. If the gods and spirits had not come to your aid recognising you as a good person, we would have had to use cows!" This was too much for me and I exploded into hysterical laughter. Andres rolled his eyes as the source of my amusement dawned on him. "Obviously the ceremony is different!" But my laughter wouldn't stop as I imagined him swinging a cow round to hit someone on top of the head.

"You were so childish. You still are at times." Andres rebuked.
"Hey, I thought you said that was a good thing?"
"Childlike NOT childish."
"Can't I be both?"
"Unfortunately you frequently are."
"I'm guessing that's not a compliment."
"What do you think?"
"I think if you had to choose your best student, I'd definitely be in the running."
"I never have favourites as you know. However if I had to choose the worst you'd definitely be in the running."

"Strangely that feels like an achievement, one to be proud of, thank you Andres."

"Not so strangely, that's exactly what I expected you to say."

"It's your shamanic gifts again, you're reading my mind." I replied mockingly and Andres obliged with feigned annoyance.

"Some shaman keep especially annoying students around. I even knew one who paid his worst student to stay. It is easy to remain centred, calm and comfortable when those things are not challenged. How we respond to irritations determines the quality of our lives; determines who we become and how we teach others by example. And so the teacher and the student are intertwined, they need one another to learn and grow."

"You need me!" I teased.

"The more we try to eliminate annoyances and irritations, or to simply avoid them, instead of learning how to deal with them gracefully, the further we get from developing those qualities that come with our growth. Qualities such as patience, understanding, tolerance, and acceptance."

"Like I said – you need me!" I laughed.

"You are exhausting!" he said holding his hands up in surrender.

All of the ceremonies were now complete and I felt quite proud of myself for having survived through it all. Apparently the rooster on his return to the cage, shared all I had told him with the chickens! What a gossip! Never trust a rooster to keep a secret. They were then taken to an open area of land where I watched them be released to carry my hopes and dreams to the world. All I saw were three chickens and a rooster stagger like four drunk men off into the wilderness. I thought this was their moment of freedom and purpose. Thanks to my veterinary friend I now know they were probably taking their last steps before dying as their air sacs had been flattened by their abdominal contents. My romantic imagery destroyed, I now have to live with the knowledge that I, a vegetarian, am at least partially (most probably) responsible for the death of three chickens and a rooster.

Walking up to me, Andres took out a small black pouch from his pocket and I was presented with my hand-woven ropes of protection. He explained they were to be worn knotted at the top of my arms at all times for one year, and thereafter whenever I sensed I was around evil! As he showed me how to knot them correctly, he added that they should not be visible to others. A country of tropical heat eleven months of the year and he was telling me to wear long sleeved tops for a year. Great! And, with that brief explanation and the usual waving of his hand to dismiss any further questioning from myself, attention was now turned to the hole in my head – something I had almost completely forgotten about in my frenzy over the chickens. But before he started there was a question that had been eating away at me since the whole egun situation had begun,

"Andres, do you know who did this to me? I mean, are you able to see that, to know who is responsible for causing me all this pain."

"Yes." Simple and understated as always came the response from Andres. I waited, expecting him to continue but he didn't.

"I want to know who it was. Tell me!" I demanded.

"No."

Never expecting he would refuse to tell me, I was somewhat taken aback. "What do you mean no? Why not? I have a right to know!"

"You have a right? A right to do what?" After a pause he continued, "To confront them? To exact revenge? What would you do with this knowledge?"

"I don't know what I would do, but I deserve to know."

"It is better not to know. The answer is less important than the reflection on what got you to this point and time. Knowledge can be dangerous when we don't know what to do with it. Knowing who did this will not change that it has been done will it? So what is the point in knowing?"

Andres' logic was infuriating. I had no idea what I would do if I knew who had set an egun loose on me. If I were honest, I'd probably do nothing but that didn't stop me wanting to know who had sought to harm me.

"Knowing how to not know is an important skill. There's always time for not knowing. Many have sought to harm you and many others will do so in the future. You cannot change that and you cannot change them. Your focus is you and only you. Don't let others dilute such an important mission. Now we must focus on closing the hole in your head so cease this chatter." With that he waved his hand dismissively at me yet again and turned away, all my questions still unanswered. I felt sick. What did he mean about others harming me? Suddenly Andres stopped and turned back to look at me, "You will know who did this to you when it is no longer important to know."

"When you realised who had done it, did you care?"

"No. Not at all." It's strange because if I had realised at any earlier time I know I would have cared. I would have said something I'm sure. It was seven years later when I realised who it had been. Not only did I not care, he was my friend and continued to be my friend. A while after that the friend started to confess to me one day and I stopped him telling me. I knew and it was no longer relevant. He had asked me why I wasn't angry with him, it was as if he wanted me to be angry and punish him so he could feel better.

"Good people do bad things sometimes. And bad people do good things. Try to remember that always with what is to come. Human nature is complex."

"That's certainly true."

"Challenging people and situations are placed on your path to serve as teachers. They help you grow and you should always be grateful. When you forgave your friend, you forgave yourself."

Andres' helpers ushered me into the mysterious room behind his desk. It was the first time I had seen what lay behind the door and I was more than a little surprised. There was no furniture in the room which was extremely large with a white tiled floor and large bay style windows with bars but no glass. In the middle of the room was a very large statue of the Virgin Mary (I was starting to have flashbacks to my Legion of Mary days) and everywhere else on the floor were all kinds of imaginable, and many more unimaginable, offerings; ranging from fruit to fully cooked meals, jewellery to toys. Apparently people came from all over to leave an offering in thanks for the work of the shaman or as a gift as part of their supplications or to leave memorabilia from what they had had resolved or cured. There were flies everywhere and the smell, though not exactly unpleasant, quickly became overpowering.

A chair was brought into the room and I was instructed to sit straight with my feet together and bow my head slightly. The helpers left and only Andres remained. The routine chanting began but this time followed by what appeared to be a conversation with someone or something I could neither see nor hear. This conversation became more heated and Andres raised his voice a few times as if he were arguing with someone. This continued for thirty minutes, all the while Andres had his hands resting on, or just above my head which felt like it was burning under the pressure, even though he was applying none. Eventually he stopped and walked around to the front of the chair. Looking at me somewhat exasperated, he asked how my hands were. This seemed like such a strange question but I then realised that my hands had turned very red and were burning. Perturbed, I gaped back at him but said nothing.

'Stay here. I'll be back shortly. You do not leave this room Maya, do you understand?" The firmness of his voice scared me a little, that and the thought of what he wasn't telling me. I nodded meekly. He left the room and I could hear a lot of discussion outside and then a car drive off. I remained seated. I don't really know why I stayed, I guess by this stage I was so far steeped in the whole process, I just accepted what was happening without question. I also had no fear of Andres and what he did. I found him immensely irritating, confusing, mystifying, but also likeable. Moreover I instinctively and unquestioningly trusted him.

Time passed and I started to think they had forgotten me. I debated getting up to have a look around, but then I remembered the strange firmness in Andres' voice before he had left. Over an hour had passed before I finally heard a car pull up. A few minutes later Andres entered the room with two other men whom he quickly explained were also shamans. Once again I was instructed to sit straight with my feet together and head bowed. This time Andres added that I must try to keep my mouth shut and all comments to myself. The routine chanting began once more, this time even louder as the three of them chanted and circled me, hovering their hands above my head. And then they stopped and began discussing something in a very animated fashion but also in a language I did not recognise. This was followed by more chanting, more hovering hands and more conversation.

Finally the three shamans moved to one end of the room and continued their conversation in loud whispers, after which the two newcomers left as abruptly as they had arrived. At no time had they acknowledged or spoken with me. However on the way out both stopped to look at me and smiled, but neither said a word. Andres then approached me and with a weary shrug of his shoulders began to speak,

"I'm sorry. The head refuses to close. You can go now."

"What do you mean 'refuses'? This is ridiculous! You can't just tell me to go! Close my head now!" I was starting to panic.

"I can't. It refuses."

"Stop saying that. You have to close it…" I was nearing desperation at this point which was somewhat ironic since ten days ago I didn't know my head was open in the first place. Come to think of it I still had no idea what it meant that it was open, so I really don't know why the situation was upsetting me so much.

"I can't. I tried. We tried. The power of three. We still could not close it. Incredible. Go away now." He added dismissively, consumed in his own thoughts.

"But I don't want it open." I was beginning to sound like a whining child.

"You have no choice."

"Well I don't want it open!" I shouted back at Andres, annoyed at his manner. The weariness and stress I had been through the last ten days was clearly coming to a head.

"Sooner or later you will have to train."

"What do you mean Andres? I don't want to train, I don't want to understand this. Close it. Please Andres just close it. I want all of this over and done with. Please."

"It will not let you go."

"Close it!" I snarled at him threateningly.

"I can't. This is unusual but it is how things are to be for you. The head will not close. We have no power over such things."

"Well I don't want it!" I found this news truly disturbing, despite the fact that I had no real idea of what he was talking about.

"This is not my decision. It is your fate."

"I don't believe in fate!" I snapped back.

"You should be grateful. You have been chosen. Many seek this, you have been given a gift. Do not be so ungrateful." Although Andres had spoken in a gentle voice, I felt scolded. Then I felt angry for feeling I had done something wrong. Finally, I simply felt helpless.

"But I don't know what it means. I don't know what I'm supposed to do Andres."

"Be calm. Take care. Watch for the signs. When you are ready you will see them and you will know what to do. I will be here when you need me, when you are ready to learn. Go away now. I'm very tired."

And with that extremely unhelpful and vague attempt at advice, he left the room instructing me to spend some quiet time in contemplation of how what had occurred would change my life. I sat there contemplating how much I just wanted to go home and forget all that had happened. I contemplated how ridiculous it all was and how I believed none of it, least of all that I had some gaping spiritual hole on the crown of my head. I swore as I left that day that it was the last time I would see Andres and the last I would ever have to do with his crazy mystical world. And for a couple of years it was.

"We cannot run forever from who we are, from our true natures."

"I can try."

"It will follow you regardless. If you accept who you are then happiness will follow you…like your shadow."

"How deep." I retorted sarcastically.

"As deep as a well filled with stones."

"What the hell is that supposed to mean, it doesn't even make sense Andres. Sometimes I think you say these things to annoy me. I don't think you even know what they mean."

"I think you could be right," replied the laughing Andres, "but there is one thing you must always remember about shadows."

"What would that be?"

"Shadows cannot be broken."

VI

I left Andres' home that day believing these events would soon be forgotten and that the opening in my head (if there even really was one) would go away of its own accord. I had laughed at the idea of there being signs, what would I have been looking for anyway? But then as the months passed signs began to appear and without me ever looking for them or knowing what I was looking for. And I began to recognise them. However I also chose to remain in firm denial, choosing to ignore anything which linked me with Andres and my spiritual path.

Since that day numerous people have commented on the opening in my head which I find both incredulous and humiliating. I never know whether to admit I know or treat them as if they are mad: probably I end up doing both most of the time. Sometimes I have been discussing mysterious events or auras, but at other times I have had strangers walk up to me in the street and comment as if it is their right to do so and as if I would ever be okay with them doing so.

One year, I was out Christmas shopping and an elderly woman started stalking, literally stalking me around the shops. At first I thought it was kind of funny, although why anyone would find being stalked by an eighty year old woman funny I do not know. Four shops later I was starting to feel very uncomfortable. I decided to join the queue, buy my stuff and get out. I figured once I had my purchases, if I walked fast she probably wouldn't be able to keep up. Then I turned around and she was standing right behind me in the queue, no purchases in her basket. She just stood there staring at me. I whispered under my breath for her to go away, at which point she exclaimed for all to hear. 'Your head's open! And you know it don't you?' I was mortified and whispered at her to shut up and go away, hastily remembering to add somewhat unconvincingly that I had no idea what she was talking about. This only worsened the situation and she began shouting for all to hear about my head being open. If my head really were open, I'd have crawled into it there and then and hid for a week!

"Will you take your gran outside please, she's making a scene?" I couldn't believe the shop assistant had just asked me that.

"She's not my gran!" I snapped back.

"Okay your mum, whatever, just take her out." I glared back at the young sales assistant who met my glare with a sarcastic grin that the young often have when they believe themselves invincible.

"I don't know who she is." I said through gritted teeth, "She is not with me!"

"Yeh right. Whatever." Responded the sarcastic sales assistant.

"Where's your Christmas spirit? She's obviously with you," chirped in some annoying woman in the queue, "and you're holding us all up!"

"Poor old dear has got dementia by the looks of it." Another added.

"Where's your Christmas spirit...." But just as I was about to add some profanities the store manager and store security turned up. I should point out the old woman was still going on about my head throughout this.

"Please leave the store. Security will escort you." The manager stated looking at me in disgust.

"What the hell! What have I done? I haven't even bought my stuff yet."

"If you do not leave now we will be forced to call the police." You have to be kidding me I thought. I had done nothing and this old woman had still not shut up. Then he added, "And take your grandmother with you."

"She's not my..." What was the point? I stormed out the shop as 'gran' came after me. Outside I began to walk faster. This old woman turned out to be fairly nimble for her age and I found myself breaking into a jog. Still she followed me. I considered going faster and darting across a busy road, but didn't want her death on my conscience if she were flattened by a passing car, so I stopped and let her catch up.

"What do you want from me?" I panted, realising with considerable annoyance that I was more out of breath than her.

"Nothing."

"Nothing? Nothing! What the hell are you following me for? Are you mad?"

"I just wanted to say hello and..."

"You just wanted to say hello? Are you serious?" Four shops, three blocks and one total humiliation later and all she wanted was to say hello!

"'...and give you my blessing. You have a wonderful gift." And with that the crazy old woman walked away. I stood there in shock staring after her.

"These things happen when you ignore your true path." Andres offered when I told him. *"No Andres, these things always just happen to me! I'm a magnet for crazy people. You're a good example of that!"* I looked out the corner of my eye to see if Andres would react to my comment, but of course he didn't.

"When you ignore the path, the spirits have to find ways to communicate. When you ignore the spirits, they have to find ways to ensure you listen?"

"Can't they be more subtle?"

"They tried, I'm sure, but you ignored them. This is what happens if you ignore them. How many times do I have to tell you?"

"I'm not finding this whole process very democratic Andres." He laughed. *"So what am I supposed to do? No don't answer that. I know what you're going to say and..."*

"And you don't want to hear it."

"Now you are learning." I replied but my feeling of having got one over on Andres was short- lived.

"Yes mi hija and it would seem you are not."

I grew to accept the comments as a part of my life, if not as normal exactly. What is normal after all? Not much in my life had ever been normal. How I longed for the Legion of Mary days going round doors which had let me live a more obscure life than I was living now! I do often wonder if people would mention the hole in the head if I weren't aware of it: you know that whole chicken and egg thing. What an inadvertently appropriate analogy! What I mean is, if all of this had never happened to me, would they still approach me? And how would I react when they did approach me? These are questions destined to remain unanswered it would seem. But before I continue I think I should explain how I ended up in Arajua in the first place. Unfortunately the explanation is neither short nor simple. Come to think of it, like everything else, it's not very logical either.

Growing up with the religious fervour and strict rules of my parents had instilled in me a desire to run. Not to run anywhere in particular, just run away. I had a few unsuccessful trial attempts in my early teens. Once I packed a bag and ran away to my grandmother's house, which was a lengthy five minutes walk away. The intention is what counts. She was my beacon of normality. I remember sitting in her front room telling her all the horrific religious things I was involved in and she listened intently, nodded her head and said, "I really don't know what your father's problem is, I certainly never brought him up like that." For some reason, to this day I find that comment hilarious.

Anyway later that night I returned home, aware I wouldn't get very far on my limited budget, only to discover nobody had realised I was gone. My first big stance and attempted statement had gone unnoticed. A sign of what was to come in my adult life perhaps.

I felt trapped and was desperate to be a part of a bigger world that did not make me feel so claustrophobic. Having survived school, just about, I went on to university in the same city meaning I continued to live at home. I majored in literature as it was the only subject that I felt truly passionate about. I loved books. I loved the art of writing. And, I must give credit where it is due, my knowledge of religion and the bible actually aided me immensely in the study of literature and literary references. I sailed through university, making little to no effort. Mainly because I didn't need to, but also because I was generally a passenger in my own life. I didn't know where I was going or what I was doing. So one week after graduation I found myself at the other end of the world, in Japan, teaching English.

It was a year fraught with disappointment, all on the side of the Japanese I might add. The scheme I had signed up for took on graduates for one year as English teachers, paid very well and promised a year of excitement and adventure. They lied. I quickly learned that being a tourist in Japan is an incredible experience: living there was to be quite a different story.

For the first week I had an orientation programme in a fantastic hotel in the heart of Tokyo. All the student teachers from English speaking countries around the globe were gathered in a five-star hotel, having been flown business class to the capital Tokyo from their respective home countries. It was an auspicious start and I was convinced I had made a wonderful decision in coming here. We had a timetable of meetings and evening events and a spattering of free time to explore the city. Tokyo, at first sight was overwhelming – its cleanliness and organisation in such an over-populated city was impressive. Its curious, not to mention tasteless, modern architecture sat side-by-side with stunning traditional buildings and monuments. There was little in between, something I soon learned that was true of people's attitudes also. This was my first introduction into the 'black and white' Japanese mentality with a zero tolerance for anything in between, but I was too mesmerised to give it any proper thought.

After the first couple of meetings I got the main drift of what was going on (in my opinion) and decided to skip the rest. I did, however, with a great sense of responsibility attend breakfast, lunch and snack breaks. Only the evening meal was not provided but I stocked up for that with secret 'doggie bags' at breakfast. I would party at night, unless a buffet event was planned, and then set my alarm faithfully to rise at seven when I would shower, dress and go down for breakfast, after which I would return to bed and set my alarm for lunchtime. Most evenings were filled with buffets, traditional dance and music extravaganzas and a general introduction into the cultural aspects of Japanese society. I probably should have paid more attention but once you've heard one Japanese drum you've heard them all, and the same follows through for the dance. My ignorance betrays me I know but it really is the same everywhere, from women dancing with baskets of fruit on their heads in Arajua to Peking opera in China, after a while it all starts to look and sound the same. In Japan the thrill started to wear off quicker than I had imagined. As the week came to a close and we were forced into the reality of knowing we would all be going our separate ways into the unknown. Insecurity and fear set in and the big adventure rapidly grew less appealing.

After the week's orientation we were put on buses to travel to the region where we would be working. For some this meant another flight or long train journey but for me it was just a one-hour bus ride to a suburb of Tokyo called

Saitama. I was one of the lucky ones apparently! We were informed that on arrival at our destinations a representative of the school we would be working for would pick us up. That was the point at which it all started to go downhill with the speed of a car whose brakes had been cut! We arrived at our location where a lot of stern looking suited men were standing waiting. We were told in no uncertain terms to stay seated on the bus until our names were called so as not to cause confusion (apparently it was hard to tell us apart as we all look the same). When we heard our names we were to step forward and be claimed, like lost baggage, by our school representatives. We all sat tentatively on the bus looking out at the different shapes and sizes of people waiting to claim us, each of us trying to guess who might be picking us up. The Japanese stared back blankly, no sign of emotion – something I became very familiar with over the coming year.

Finally my name was called and I made my way slowly to the door of the bus and tried to look happy and confident to the crowd below. Nobody claimed me. Once again my name was called and once again I remained unclaimed. After this process had been repeated far too many times for comfort, I was returned to my seat, crushed, while they proceeded with the list. I sat there feeling more alone and dejected than I had ever felt in my life. Why had no one come to pick me up? What would happen to me? Where would they take me now? I stared out the window as the crowd of waiting representatives grew smaller and smaller. With nobody else left on the bus I was called to the front and my name hollered one last time. Looking out I could only see the organisers who had accompanied us and, leaning against a car to the side of the bus, a middle-aged man who had been there from the start; smoking, staring at the ground and shuffling his feet uncomfortably.

My name was called again this time with the name of my school. Nobody came forward at first, then slowly the smoker reluctantly dragged himself over explaining that he was the representative from my school. More than a little deflated, not to mention insulted and humiliated, by his whole attitude I asked why he had not come forward earlier as I had seen him standing there. He shrugged and explained with a weary sigh of disappointment that he had hoped if he hadn't come forward to claim me, they might have offered him someone else! Seeing the look of confusion on my face, he explained they had been hoping for a blonde! My year in Japan was off to a great start!

We loaded my luggage in the trunk of his car and set off on the journey to my town which, he explained, was approximately ninety minutes away. While part of me felt I should make an effort to converse with him, another part was still smarting at his attempt to leave me in the 'lost and found' section of the Japanese education department. We sat in silence for thirty minutes. The silence was finally broken when Hosaka, as I eventually learned was his name, suggested we stop for lunch. I readily agreed hoping that it would help to break the ice a little. I should have known not even a pickaxe would have succeeded with that task.

At the restaurant we were shown into a cubicle with a knee-high table and, after removing our shoes, were handed steaming hot cloths to clean our hands and face. I attempted to find a comfortable position in which to eat, breathe and talk all at the same time. I failed. Realizing no such position existed I decided to just cross my legs much to the horror of Hosaka who quickly informed me that while I may choose to dress in a masculine fashion (Excuse me?), it was not acceptable that I sit in one. Apparently as a female I was required to kneel, unless otherwise instructed by my male host. Hosaka clearly took delight in my discomfort and had no intention of inviting me to sit in a more comfortable position.

Forcing a friendly smile I knelt, albeit torturously, determined to show that I could and was in no pain

84

whatsoever. After about fifteen minutes the pain did cease: as did all sensation in my lower extremities. I opened the menu which, not surprisingly, I didn't understand a word of. Hosaka waited, watching me with an amused look, for what seemed like an interminable period of time before informing me that he would be ordering for both of us. I thanked him and mentioned to please bear in mind that I was vegetarian. I might just as well have said I was the daughter of Satan judging by his horrified reaction.

"But you eat fish of course!" he stated rather than asked.

"No." I replied meekly.

"Are you sick?"

"No."

"What is wrong with you then?" He asked accusingly with a look of complete and utter confusion, if not anger, on his face.

"Nothing." I replied, equally confused.

"Well this is not good. Your host family will not like this. It is very inconsiderate and selfish of you." I stared back speechless as he continued, "Why can't you just pick the meat out of your food?'

"Because..."

"You are a disappointment!" he said cutting me off. I was lost for words for many reasons but just as I was recovering my composure he sent me reeling once again. "What kind of foreigner are you? Your hair is dark. Your eyes are dark. I think you are trying to copy Japanese. You don't eat meat. You're not American. AND you have small breasts!" Wow! The list of complaints had been bad enough, but the last one had thrown me for a loop. I wasn't quite sure which feature disappointed him the most but I was guessing the breasts were at the top of the list. Now let me just say that while my breasts are not of a size that might rate me well in a porn movie, they are not exactly small so I'm not sure what he had been expecting. Well actually I think I have a pretty good idea what he was expecting and it was the result of too many pay-per-view films he'd clearly been watching! Once again I was unsure how to respond and found myself staring back in an almost apologetic way for my obvious shortcomings. I took a deep breath and prayed that Hosaka was not representative of the other Japanese I would be dealing with. God saw fit to ignore my prayers, a little unfair considering my childhood piety, enforced as it may have been. Perhaps it was punishment for my generous self-payments for my Christmas nativity duties. The revenge of Baby Jesus.

Lunch finally arrived. A cold soup with lots of thick noodles and a raw egg on top. I stared at it for a while determining how I would navigate the less appealing parts, which was about all of it from where I was sitting and that was when I heard it – the noise that was to haunt my meal times for the next year and echo through my nightmares for years to come – the slurping! I should explain I am noise sensitive. I would like to say I am just sensitive but according to those around me it is abnormal and I seem to hear and get upset by things that only someone with bionic powers could possibly hear. For years I had complained to my family as we sat around the dinner table that they ate too loudly, slurped their soup, spoke with their mouths half full, breathed too loudly and now I was paying back a karmic debt for my intolerance – paying it back tenfold. Without realising it, I had come to the land of the rising sun where slurping, burping, farting, nose picking and numerous other bodily functions that should only ever be carried out in private, were not only tolerated, but actually encouraged as correct social behaviour.

Hosaka would lift the start of a noodle from his soup and slurp it up until the tail end splashed off his upper lip (and occasionally across the table at me). I meanwhile was trying furiously to cut the noodles daintily with my chopsticks and lift them in safe portions to my mouth. Needless to say I was not making much progress and the raw egg was now mingling with the other elements of my cold soup. Hosaka then informed me in disgust that my eating habits were not only rude but also off-putting to watch! How ironic! He told me that slurping was a form of appreciation and failure to do so was an insult to my host. There were clearly many rules I needed to learn about and fast; I should have paid more attention at my week's orientation. Slowly I attempted to slurp my noodles, despite not feeling in any way appreciative, with the ends splashing off my cheeks and occasionally into my eyes. After about ten minutes of this agony, and having spilt and splashed more soup than I had actually consumed, I looked at Hosaka in desperation and asked if I could be excused for not finishing my food, as I was full. In reality I had consumed very little but as my appetite had been killed in the attempt to eat, I preferred not to continue. Hosaka muttered something under his breath and then told me it was time to leave. For the rest of the drive Hosaka asked me some extremely personal questions about my life, my work experience and my habits. He was unimpressed with everything I told him. I asked him some questions about his life but he was reticent about responding. Over my year there I learned quite quickly that while the Japanese felt it was their right to know absolutely everything about my life past and present, they felt it was an invasion of their privacy for me to ask about theirs. I was not Japanese (something I was never allowed to forget) and clearly different rules applied. Then just as we drove up to the host family house where I was to spend the next two months, he turned and informed me that nobody in the family spoke English.

My new family had been eagerly awaiting my arrival and came rushing to the door at which point their looks of excitement rapidly turned to ones of disappointment. A look I was quickly becoming familiar with. My host father greeted me cordially and then entered into a lengthy discussion with Hosaka of which I was clearly the sole topic. Eventually with my visitor slippers provided, I was shuffled into what appeared to be a living room area and instructed to sit. They asked, through my translator, if I would like coffee and cake, which I eagerly accepted upon which they all shuffled off to the kitchen where more deep discussions ensued. I asked Hosaka at this point what all the talking was about. I wasn't sure he would tell me but he gleefully replied.

"They are very disappointed. You are not American. You do not have blonde hair and blue eyes. And your breasts are very small." The breasts again! "At least you have a big nose." A back handed compliment if ever I heard one.

"What were they expecting?" I don't know why I asked as the clear answer appeared to be anyone but me.

"Your predecessor was blonde. She had blue eyes and large breasts. She was American and very friendly. We liked her. We are very sad she has gone. We are very sad with her replacement." Over the next year I was frequently told about the blonde blue-eyed American with her admirable breasts! I can only assume she quit to pursue her movie career as an adult film actress!

Over coffee the atmosphere lightened slightly as they became resigned to the fact that they had a dark haired, dark eyed, disappointingly endowed non-American for the next year. After some more confabulations they presented me with a welcome gift. Hosaka immediately volunteered the information that I should bow in thanks and that I must always bow lower than anyone older or more respected than me. In my entire year in Japan it seemed nobody was ever younger or less respected than me, at least according to Hosaka who would have had my chin scraping off the ground constantly if he could. This man detested me and he could not, or simply would not, hide it.

The beautifully wrapped gift lay in front of me and trembling with anticipation I slowly began to unwrap it.

After various layers I found a box and inside the box was a tube-shaped wooden doll with a loose head. The head, which I realised was removable – after initially thinking I had broken it - was attached to a long thin piece of wood with a small curve at the end. Remembering my manners I thanked them profusely while Hosaka laughed and commented that I clearly didn't know what it was. At this point he took it on himself to explain the purpose of my gift. Apparently you placed the stick part in your ear, the rest was for purely decorative and storage purposes, and moved it around so that the curvy bit could scrape away any excess wax (and perhaps burst your ear drum in the process). The pleasure of this experience, he continued to explain, was immeasurable. At this point he obviously mistook my look of horror for one of confusion and swiftly grabbed the stick from my hand, telling me to watch while he showed me how it worked. Before I could object half of my new ear picker disappeared into his right ear. Eventually he removed it to display a small ball of yellow ear wax which he shifted from the stick onto the sofa. As I looked on appalled, he passed the stick to me and urged me to try for myself. I wanted to cry.

Over the next few days I tried to become accustomed to life with my host family. They trialled lots of new and interesting food on me. Hosaka had broken the devastating news about me being a vegetarian and, fully respecting my wishes, they served me lots of vegetables unfortunately with the meat hidden underneath. I believe they actually thought if I couldn't see it, I would eat it. And every time I lifted the food to remove the meat, they would look surprised as if they had no idea how it could have possibly got there. The month of August was the time during which Japan and I would become acquainted with one another. My Japanese family were kind and considerate but the strain of living under the same roof as them was almost unbearable. They took me everywhere to show me off to their friends, I had no privacy (an alien concept to most Japanese) and I longed to have an English conversation with someone, anyone. There was also the strain of always being so polite and trying to do the 'right' thing. In my whole life I had never made this much effort with my own family.

Without even realising most of the time, I made mistake after mistake which either produced shocked gasps or incessant giggles. I pointed my chopsticks east instead of west; walked barefoot on the tatami mats; wore my toilet slippers in the dining room; walked in the hallway with my shoes on; crossed my legs when I should have knelt; didn't bow low enough; looked people in the eye; blew my nose in public; failed to slurp or burp my appreciation of my food; didn't peel grapes and apples and insisted on only eating eggs if they had been cooked; I also refused to bathe in the same bath water that my host father had finished with (it was an honour they told me that I was getting to use it second); I wore the wrong colour of clothing...and this is just a small sample from the catalogue of my crimes. But without doubt my greatest crimes were not being American, not having blonde hair and blue eyes, and not having porn star sized breast implants. And how could I forget, not eating meat.

After two months I moved to a one room apartment in a neighbouring town. My homestay family continued to visit, frequently. The town I moved to was small but situated near a railway station. It was a forty-minute train ride to the heart of Tokyo which proved my escape line on many occasions from the suburban nightmare in which I lived and in which everyone knew what I was up to, often before I did. I had refused an apartment on the bottom floor after hearing stories of the problems with giant cockroaches. Nobody had told me they could fly. My apartment was a three-minute walk from the railway station and the trains regularly caused my apartment to vibrate, drowning out the television, my saviour. There were four programmes in

English every week: Knightrider, Baywatch, Little House on the Prairie and the news. I watched them all faithfully and repeatedly. What can I say? It was a lonely year at times and David Hasselhoff was there for me when nobody else was!

On a Monday and Tuesday I went to a local coeducational school where I had no schedule and sometimes taught and sometimes (most of the time) sat and read books, before sneaking home when nobody was looking, in time for Knightrider. Wednesday to Friday I worked in an all girls' school for low achievers and trust me they had truly earned that title. My students were not studious and they certainly were not dedicated, but the majority were fun. This was my main school and where my 'caretaker' Hosaka worked. On weekends I was free much to the disgust of the Japanese teachers who had to work on a Saturday.

In September all Japanese students return to school for the start of their second term regardless of the day on which it falls. This year it fell on a Saturday. This was to be my big day – the day I had eagerly been anticipating for over a month. I was told to arrive for 8am and go immediately to the school principal's office. This I duly did and was shown into an empty room and left for the next thirty minutes until the principal breezed through the door announcing that it was 'time'. Our first stop was the teachers' meeting where I sat next to the principal and witnessed full on the general disappointment that spread around the room as people saw me for the first time. I know – dark hair, dark eyes, breasts too small – I could read their minds by now, perhaps the hole in my head had already kicked into action giving me the gift of mind reading. Although I think the gift was undoubtedly supported by the clear disappointment on the face of everyone I met. Well that and the fact that they told me in no uncertain terms to my face at every possible opportunity. You have no idea how many times I witnessed that look of disappointment or, even worse, the number of times I was shouted at on turning round for trying to 'trick' people into thinking I was Japanese from behind because of my long dark hair! People actually thought I was trying to fool them into thinking I was Japanese and were outraged by it.

Anyway I had prepared a little introductory speech in Japanese thinking this would be a good move to ingratiate myself with my colleagues. This was received in typical Japanese fashion – with no reaction whatsoever. I then proceeded to say a few more words in English, a language perhaps six other people in the room understood. For this I received a standing ovation. Next it was on to the assembly hall to meet the students and yet another speech. This was followed by another assembly, this time with the parents and yet another speech. I was rapidly learning that the Japanese loved their speeches which usually went on way beyond my will to live. My official translator for these speeches was usually Hosaka, who had informed me it was insulting for me to speak Japanese when people came to hear me speak English (even if they couldn't understand a word of it), and he rarely translated anything I actually said, of that I am sure.

The aim behind the teaching programme I was on, was to promote team-teaching with Japanese English teachers in classes. It is intended as an opportunity for the students to hear English as it is spoken by native speakers and to promote the usage of everyday English among the teachers whose English speaking skills are often minimal. In the year I was there I rarely team taught. Most of the time I went to classes alone or turned up for a class that had been cancelled, unbeknownst to me, only to find I had no students. Nobody ever informed me in advance. My duties were minimal and many of the Japanese English teachers tried to avoid me as they were embarrassed by their own English speaking skills or lack thereof. Hosaka continued to be unfriendly and critical and would often talk about me in the staffroom while I was sitting there. Although I could never be sure I rapidly learned to say, 'I know what you are saying about me!' in Japanese, which frequently left him embarrassed and apologetic. When I worked with the students at the start they frequently repeated a phrase over and over to me 'zenzen wakarimasen deshita'. I took this to be a complimentary phase about my teaching but soon learned it actually meant 'We have understood nothing!' This was to be my motto for the year. They understood nothing and, to be honest, neither did I.

After the final lessons every day the students would clean the school. What a fantastic system! Can you imagine trying to implement that in the UK? In Japan no cleaners are hired for the schools and it is regarded as the duty of the students to ensure that the school is clean and tidy and a source of personal pride to them. Every day the students clean the classrooms, staffrooms, offices and even the toilets. When the school grounds need tidied, it is the students once again who see to this, from picking up litter to weeding. With this completed it is time for their club activities. All students without fail must join a club and it is regarded as every teacher's duty to take charge of one club at least, irrelevant of whether or not they actually know anything about it. The logical step would have been for me to take the English club but one of the Japanese English teachers already had that role and obviously had no intention of giving it up. Probably because, as I later learned, all they did was watch movies. As a result I ended up in the Kendo club! Kendo (aka the way of the sword) is the modern Japanese martial art of sword-fighting: physically and mentally challenging combining strong martial art skills and values with sport-like physical elements. They also had really cool outfits. As I enthusiastically turned up on my first day, my instructor removed his mask to greet me. It was Hosaka.

Looking back it seems like I spent half of the year introducing myself. Every new class I taught, every workshop, every orientation meeting, every community gathering, every party, and every official occasion I was required to introduce myself and give a speech. I bored myself to tears. After a while I started to change information about myself and add unbelievable facts but nobody ever reacted, few had any idea what I was saying and when Hosaka translated he made up his own version every time anyway. Often I felt the situation was hopeless and usually I was right. The disappointment at me not being American was profound and they constantly criticised my non-American pronunciation and spelling. Some students comfortingly told me they preferred my English and wanted to learn good 'King's English' like mine. I hadn't the heart to tell them we hadn't had a king for a very long time.

There was however one teacher, Komatsu, a part time art teacher and illustrator of children's books who became my friend. He never judged or criticised me. Repeatedly he defended me to those who did. His paintings were beautiful, all the more amazing because his hands were crippled and deformed from rheumatoid arthritis. In many ways he was my Japanese grandfather, gently scolding me when I did wrong or felt too frustrated to keep going and pushing me to be the best I was capable of being each day I wanted to run away and never come back. The day I left Japan he told me that we would always be friends. He then told me that I needed to know that he was dying and had been given only a few months to live. He lived for almost a year after I left: word of his death reaching me during my first month in South America. All that was good in Japan, all my best memories, are embodied in him.

That year in Japan was the first step of moving constantly over the years to come, searching for a place to belong and in the process becoming more alienated from everyone and everything. I searched for that sense of belonging in the most obscure places and each time realised I was destined to be an outsider. In my life I have travelled so much of the world and seen so many things – good and bad. I have experienced extremes of betrayal and loyalty, of love and hate. I have seen and heard things that have given me nightmares and others that have aroused the most beautiful dreams from within. And I believe I am a fortunate person for I have retained the most optimistic belief in a world I have seen at its darkest.

"The teachers in our lives can take many forms. You travelled searching for an illusion. If you try to live on illusion, you will die of disillusion."

"Or hunger." I joked but Andres was in one of his more serious moods.

"We write our own stories you and I. And we help others to write theirs. But never forget that the spirits write on crooked lines."

"Andres I really don't know what you are talking about. What is that supposed to mean even?" My irritation levels were rising, "Sometimes I think I never know what you are talking about. How many times do I have to tell you that?"

"Yes I know." Came Andres' abrupt response.

"Well that's not very helpful!"

"All those travels. All those experiences. You were given chances to learn."

"I know and you're going to tell me I wasted all those opportunities, that I learned nothing." Even though I rarely understood Andres' cryptic lessons, I hated the thought that I had disappointed him.

"No mi hija. You learned a great deal, you just don't know it yet. When the time is right, the learning will reveal itself to you."

"And when will that be."

"Soon. Be patient. Use the skills you have developed. You know a good guitarist will play on one string." I looked

up infuriated by Andres' riddles, only to find him looking directly at me with a grin on his face.

"Don't you ever get tired of playing with me?"

"Does an elephant get tired of carrying his trunk?"

I wanted to punch him in the face.

VII

Coming from the airport late on my first night in Arajua I remember looking around thinking the country looked somewhat like India: Calcutta to be precise. Alarm bells should have sounded at that alone, but it was dark and I was tired, not to mention still incredibly naive and stupid. When my year in Japan had finally come to an end I convinced some friends I had made to travel with me to India (only because I didn't want to go alone, though it may have been the better option). I don't know why, but it was an idea in my head that I needed to see India and that it would be the most incredible trip. I blame my love of literature for many of my insane travels. People romanticise or flat out lie in books. Except me of course! The books I read always told of great adventures, not the misadventures that frequently happened to me. My friends, and I use that term loosely, were not convinced India was the smartest choice of destination. However they finally agreed, on the proviso that I took care of the organisation side of things, something they seemed to forget in the retrospective casting up I had to listen to afterwards.

On a strict budget I found us cheap tickets flying into Calcutta. Of course I had heard stories about the place, Mother Teresa and all that (remember that Catholic background), but the truth is my geographical awareness and navigational skills are questionable at best. I figured we would get a cheap flight in and then we start travelling around by train. It all sounded so romantic. When Indian friends screwed up their faces in an expression of horror that anyone in their right mind would fly into Calcutta, I dismissed it as an exaggeration, reassuring myself that it would be a day or two at most and then we would move on.

How bad could it be I asked myself? The fact that the trip ended early and I friendless answers that!

There were four of us who had all been on the same one-year teaching programme in Japan. In my defence I never especially liked any of them in the first place. Clara knew me well and we had experienced a few other travels together: in other words she should have known better. A mental check at that stage would have reminded both of us how traumatic some of those earlier trips had often been. Sara and I did not get on and never had. Her American enthusiasm and comments on my 'quaint' accent had been driving me mad for months and I had warned Clara not to invite her under any circumstances. Unfortunately that warning had arrived about twenty minutes too late and Sara had been ecstatic at the idea of joining us on our travels. Libby didn't really speak much, probably because she couldn't get a word in edgeways around Sara. She later revealed that it terrified her to travel with me because I was 'an accident waiting to happen'. Bloody cheek!

On arrival at the airport in Calcutta – did I say airport? Oh how loosely I use that term – I was robbed. I hadn't even made it through customs yet! I did take up chase, especially as I had been relieved of a very expensive camera given to me as a graduation present by my parents. My fellow travellers hysterically pleaded with me to just let it go. My thieving attacker seemed to agree on that point and with no intention of running in the scorching heat (the customs queue where I had been robbed was on a disused runway) soon stopped in his path and turned around to face me. This is where my lack of considering consequences shows itself all too clearly; what was I thinking I would do if I caught up with him?

He looked at me smiling, quite friendly for a thief I have to say, and held up the camera bag with one hand saying, "You want this?". I thought, "How pleasant all I had to do was ask for my belongings to be returned." He repeated,

"You want this?" this time flicking open a knife with his other hand "Then you get this!". Hmm let me consider this one for a while. The guilt at my carelessness in having this expensive gift stolen dissipated rapidly, although a part of me kept saying, "You are in the secure part of the airport surely someone will help you, like maybe the police who are standing around watching!" But alas nobody was coming to my aid, or seemed to have any intention of doing so. Defeated I shrugged my shoulders and turned to walk away at which point the thief called for me to stop. I turned elated at the thought his conscience had got the better of him and he was going to return the camera after all. As I turned round he threw the camera case at me. "You can have that!" he shouted still with that same friendly smile. He had of course removed the camera.

As I returned to my friends they already had that look of irritation with me, the look I know only too well of "Why can't you just keep your mouth shut?" or "Why can't you just let things be?". But I had bought and read my traveller's guide to India (well bits of it anyway, clearly not the section on Calcutta) and I knew robberies were common in India (not necessarily before you get through customs at the airport right enough). The book encouraged one not to be put off this beautiful and fascinating country should such a fate befall you. One was not put off. I was determined; I would enjoy India if it killed me. As it turns out it almost did.

Calcutta was all any sane person might have imagined; filthy, with extreme poverty, lepers and rats the size of cats...and that was the best of it. We followed the recommendations of the guidebook (the fact that the guidebook recommended a particular area where you could view 'the largest rats' ever seen in their hordes should have been a warning sign that the hotel recommendations may not be the best) and headed to one of the central hotels in a taxi. This vehicle had no cushions on its back seat, only open springs and our taxi driver drove like a maniac as we bounced up and down on the springs, rapidly developing haemorrhoids. The former was the guide's recommendation, not the latter. At first when the driver informed us we had reached our destination I thought he had misunderstood the address, or had taken us to some unsafe place to rob us. But no, we were in the city centre and my heart rapidly transferred to the pit of my stomach and stayed there for the next few weeks. I think it was at that moment that I first fully embraced a sense of total fear that was not to leave me until the day I stepped off the plane in Thailand. Looking back I find it funny that I ever could have been so afraid. Perhaps India was my initiation into fear that somehow removed any proper sense of it in events that happened thereafter. It was as if I had this new idea in my head that I had become untouchable after India, convinced that after that experience I could handle anything anyone threw at me. Whatever, it did set me in good stead for what was to follow, there's no denying that.

Calcutta went from bad to worse and did so rapidly. It was difficult to get a hotel room and when we did it was already dark and the famous power cuts were occurring frequently. India, like so much of South America, experiences frequent power cuts that can last from minutes to hours to days. In Arajua I learned to live with this and did in fact accept it as normal; in Calcutta they were terrifying as you were thrown into a pit of darkness with no glimmer of light in sight. Our hotel had air conditioning (when there was electricity), a large bathroom with a shower, stained sheets, no lock on the door and rats which we could hear scratching around the room all night in the interminable darkness. This proved to be one of the better hotels we stayed at in India.

During one of the power cuts we sat discussing the trip and looking at the funny side of all of it – well I may have been the only one capable of seeing the funny side at that stage – and came to the decisions that,

a) we would get a train to Delhi in the morning and exit Calcutta as fast as possible, never to return

b) if, horror of horrors, we could not for any reason accomplish a, we would move hotels

c) I would never be allowed to plan a trip again.

A little harsh in my opinion but there's no reasoning with some people. The next morning I ventured out to the train station alone, having been abandoned by my 'friends' who claimed that since I had got us into this nightmare, I should be the one to get us out. I quickly consulted the trusted guidebook which had many and varied warnings about Calcutta and the train station in particular. Actually, I had started reading it rather desperately earlier that morning and was beginning to wish I hadn't. It warned of the begging lepers who would grab on to your legs and how you should just keep walking, ignoring them the best you could; it spoke of the offers of tea at the train station waiting room that would be laced with drugs so you would pass out and could be easily robbed; and it warned of the taxi drivers who would take you to unknown destinations where gangs would rob and beat you, leaving you for dead. I was beginning to wish I had never bought the damn guidebook, far less read it. I mean it all sounded a bit pessimistic to me. Sometimes not knowing is simply better. I just kept telling myself surely it couldn't be that bad. But it could.

A couple of hours later I found myself striding rapidly away from the train station with a legless leper relentlessly holding on to my ankle and bobbing up and down behind me. I had just been told that the next train to Delhi with available seats was two days away and suddenly I wasn't feeling so good. I had turned down four cups of tea, was getting plenty of strange looks and figured that a taxi back to the hotel was the best option. After all it was a toss up between being drugged and robbed, or driven to a remote location and beaten. Six of one half a dozen of the other as they say. The taxi seemed the wisest choice under the circumstances, so I flagged one down and climbed in while trying to shake of the leper whose grip and ability to bounce was disturbingly impressive. In the end (please don't judge me - I gently pushed him in the face with my free foot (calling it a kick is perhaps a little harsh) and quickly shut the door before he bounced back, against the window his hand sliding down as he slumped to the ground. I felt safe, well safer, in the taxi and breathed a sigh of relief, until a man pushing a cart hit the taxi when we had stopped at lights, infuriating the driver enough to reverse into the cart, over the man and then proceed to the hotel as if nothing had happened.

"Aren't you going to stop?" I screeched at the taxi driver.

"Why?"

"You just ran over that man!"

"So?"

"So! He might be dead!"

"So."

"That's ...that's murder..."

"Well he's probably not dead."

"He might be!"

"He might not be."

"Shouldn't we check?'

"No. Busy schedule. No time."

"But.."

"Do you want to go back? I drop you off."

"Erm no...I mean..." I don't know what I meant but I certainly wasn't going back there alone.

"Please be quiet lady. You hurt my head."

I sat there horrified that I had just not only witnessed a hit and run, but was also potentially a part of it. I looked behind me continually expecting the police to take chase and arrest me. I hadn't read anything in the guidebook about Indian prisons but based on my experiences so far I can't imagine they would be a positive experience. But the police never took chase, I doubt the police did anything at all to be honest. I learned very quickly how cheap life can be in poor countries. Something that horrified and terrified me, yet became commonplace in so many of the places I visited. Life is cheap when you are poor. Sadly it is a horrific reality of the world in which we live.

My unpopularity with my friends increased as I explained we were stuck in Calcutta for two days, while simultaneously cleaning the handprint the leper had left round my ankle and wondering whether or not leprosy was contagious. I am sure in my childhood I had read somewhere in the bible that it was, which incidentally, was the only place I had ever come across lepers. Well there and in Graham Greene novels. And I am sure they all died in his books and that it was highly contagious. Not being Jesus, I had no desire to sustain contact with any leper, contagious or not and I really don't care how un-Christian that is. I opted to leave out the fact that I may be wanted by the police as an accessory to murder, for fear that it would not go down well with my friends at this time.

We agreed to change hotels and that upping our budget for a better hotel might be a wise investment. A few blocks away was a famous colonial grand house (well, it was famous in Calcutta according to my guidebook) that had been renovated and converted into a hotel. It was praised for its large clean rooms and secure fencing around the perimeter (to keep the beggars/lepers/thieves/murderers out), which sold it to us, and so we packed up and made our move. The lady at the hotel was lovely and welcoming, extremely sympathetic to our plight and pointed out some interesting places we could visit, as well as the local Hare Krishna's where we could get clean vegetarian food. How I came to love the Hare Krishna's in India – I'd have joined them if they'd asked. Strangely enough they never did which is quite insulting considering the fact that they try to pick up anyone and everyone they can everywhere else.

There now seemed to be light at the end of the tunnel and I believed our trip might be saved after all. The following morning we awoke, a little late, to a wonderful breakfast (our standards had dropped, it was tea and toast). Some strange noises had kept us awake into the middle of the night. We sat on the patio as the lepers threw themselves against the twelve-foot iron gates pleading for money and we smiled at the thought that the next day we would be on a train away from this nightmare place. Our hostess asked if we had slept well and we commented on the strange noises. She apologised profusely and said she had forgotten to tell us that her satanic group had a meeting last night and that must have been the noise. Rewind! What?

Oblivious to our looks of horror as we weighed up tossing our luck with the lepers rather than staying there a moment longer, she proceeded to explain that she belonged to a group of Satan worshippers and that it was her week to have the meetings. They were meeting again tonight and she wondered if we would like to join them. I quickly explained that as 'practising Christians' I did not think that would be a good idea – okay practising may have been a slight exaggeration but I, for one, was certainly about to start. She shrugged and said it was up to us, we were more than welcome and there would be plenty of food and drink there. Now tempted as I was at the thought of a good meal, even I have my limits. But I was impressed by how friendly and welcoming the Satanists appeared to be and wondered, briefly, if it was worth considering joining them as part of my new spiritual adventure.

My friends hated me even more now, blaming me for yet another poor choice of hotel. A little unfair I thought, as they had been thrilled to stay there till they had discovered we might all need exorcised by the end of the trip. After some discussion and a few unsuccessful phone calls to find alternative hotels, we all agreed to stay there for the last night, all together in the same room – our solidarity and strength in numbers being an obvious obstacle for the Prince of Darkness should he come knocking. In the meantime, to take everyone's mind off of our disastrous trip, I had planned a bus tour of the city culminating in a visit to the area where Mother Teresa worked, also famous for having the largest rats ever seen. Okay perhaps not the top of anyone's list of 'places to see' on holiday but trust me there's not a lot to do in Calcutta that doesn't involve being robbed, Satan worshippers, lepers or rats. I thought I was doing a pretty good job of putting together our daily excursions.

That night we spent huddled in one room, holding any cross we could get our hands on and/or make and singing hymns from our school days. It must have worked as Satan's followers left us alone and the next morning we headed off to the train station to get the all day and all night, slowest train in the world to Delhi. They didn't tell us the all-day, all night aka 24-hour train ride was actually a three days and three nights trip. Of course the train would have gone a lot faster had people not pulled the emergency cord any time we were near their home so they could get off!

We began that train journey full of hope, we were leaving Calcutta, things could only get better . . . surely? We were split up into different compartments, Clara and I being placed with an elderly Indian couple who stared at us a lot but did not speak. We laughed and giggled: a sense of freedom and relief to be leaving Calcutta had made us temporarily giddy. As night drew close the couple opposite us pulled out some chains, which they wrapped around their luggage, and then the man padlocked the chain around his hand. I watched a little bemused. The man looked back at me equally bemused, until finally he spoke,

"Why are you not putting chains on your bag?"

"Why would I?" I asked confused.

"People will steal your bags while you sleep. Chain will keep them safe."

"But why chain them to your arm and not the chair?"

"More secure. You will feel any movement."

"We are on a train, surely we will not get robbed on a moving train."

"You are in India." No further explanation required as I had a flashback to my arrival in the airport.

Swiftly Clara jumped to the upper bunk and feigned sleep. The now very talkative gentleman informed me he had some extra chains and would help to chain me to all our bags. I agreed. I know, I know, but at the time you just think this all seems normal. In my life things like this ARE normal. When you live through things you behave in a way that with hindsight you realise you should have questioned at the very least. After it taking a considerable time to chain me intricately to our few bags, I was starting to wonder if this was the setting for a sadomasochistic porn movie (not that I'd know what that is incidentally). Eventually I fell asleep, pushing any concerns to the back of my mind as usual, only to be violently shaken awake by the strange man opposite me. He was extremely flustered and had awakened everyone in the compartment in his hushed hysteria.

"Are you a crazy girl?" he hissed. Well there is no easy answer to that question so I opted for a shrug of the shoulders and silence. "You must keep your arm tucked under you!"

"Why?" I stared back bemused and stunned from being awoken so abruptly.

"Your arm crazy girl!" he shouted pointing at my arm in response to my blank look, "Your arm!" Repetition was not clarifying the matter and he was starting to irritate me. Frustrated at my lack of understanding he shouted, "Your arm is lying at your side!" This explained nothing, after all where else would my arm be? Over the years of my extreme misadventures I have learned that people tend to state things to me as if I should know, as if it were blatantly obvious and I am some kind of idiot for not knowing what they assume I should. This was one such case. I shrugged again, his pleading look rapidly changing to one of extreme concern although I had no clear idea why.

"They will come in to steal your bags. They will see your arm and just cut your hand off!" He was acting this out for added effect and with what I can only describe as unnecessary bloodthirsty enthusiasm. "Hide your arm under your body. Like this. Harder to cut off!" He concluded with an animated sweeping action with an imaginary hatchet. This was followed by pulling his sleeve down, as he pretended he had lost his hand and cried in shock and agony. I assume this was intended to represent me. This would have been hilarious were I not the protagonist in this situation. I didn't sign up for this and there was nothing in my bag worth losing my hand for. In fact it was mainly full of dirty washing, plus an empty camera case I hadn't had the heart to dispose of. Nor did I care about Clara's bag, especially as Clara was still pretending to be asleep and trust me, nobody could possibly have slept through the theatrics that had just taken place.

"Unlock the chains." I managed in a small croaky voice, "Now!"

"But your bags?" the man queried confused.

"I don't care! They can take the bags."

"Foolish foreign girl." He grunted unimpressed by my decision as he unlocked the chains, "They are my chains. I am taking them back," he added grumpily, as if for some bizarre reason he thought I'd been hoping to keep them. "Why you such coward?"

"What?" This mad man just called me a coward after acting out me getting my hand cut off and then screaming and hopping around the train while blood spurted leading (in his dramatic version) to such extreme blood loss that I died, slumped on the floor holding my neck (for reasons unknown) with my one remaining hand. "I don't care about my bags!" I hissed at him.

"Well no crying when they go walkabout you foolish girl."

"I won't don't worry!" I replied somewhat aggressively as I pushed the chains back in his direction.

"Foolish girl." He repeated what he seemed to consider my name as his wife awoke and they discussed in Hindi what had just happened. Although speaking in Hindi every time he referred to me he would point and say 'foolish girl' in English, undoubtedly for my benefit. I spent the rest of the night awake and alert, ready and willing to hand over everyone's bags to anyone who came looking. In fact I almost hoped someone would come so I could invite them to take our co-passengers' bags.

Delhi, when we eventually arrived, was an improvement on Calcutta – a slight improvement. The rats were just as prevalent, the beggars more so, the lepers a little less. A win win situation all round based on our progress so far. Things were not looking up on the friendship front and arguments had increased in frequency along with demands that I should contact the airline and get our departure brought forward. Then, five days into our stay in Dehli, in a town near Madras, a leading member of parliament was assassinated and all hell broke loose. One of the first suicide bombings of its kind, it killed the member of parliament and fifteen others. The country was thrown into chaos and we were told by the embassy that we needed to head back to our point of arrival – Calcutta – and exit the country as fast as possible. Our flights were rearranged to leave two days later and once again we found ourselves on a train heading back to a city we had all sworn we would never set foot in again.

While this all may seem incidental, it does however attest to my ability to be in the wrong place at the wrong time, something I have unwittingly mastered the art of. But let's not get ahead of ourselves. One disaster at a time is enough for all of us.

"*You attract these events to you.*"

"*Tell me something I don't know*"

"*It is because your head is open.*" *Andres replied nonchalantly.*

"*Well we all know the solution for that.*" *I retorted annoyed.*

"*We have been through this repeatedly. We tried, it will not close. You must learn to control what you attract.*"

"*If I could do that, I'd have found Mr. Right by now don't you think?*" *I scoffed.*

"*Not what I meant Maya, as you well know.*"

"*You're blaming me for all these incidents and all the crazy people who come into my life?*"

"*Yes.*" *That was not the answer I was expecting.*

"*How is it my fault?*" *I hissed with incredulity.*

"*You are very irresponsible with the opening in your head.*"

"*My mouth?*" *I offered jokingly.*

"*That too.*" *Andres shot back with a serious look.*

"*I don't know what you mean.*"

"*That is a lie. He who knows nothing, doubts nothing. You do not doubt the truth of my words.*"

"*Do you have a great saying about she who understands nothing, cos I have no idea what you're talking about...*"

"*Not at present.*"

"*Any other pearls of wisdom you'd like to share Andres?*"

"*A hatchet in the mouth is more harmful than a hatchet in the hand. It will serve you well to remember that.*"

"*What?*" *I had no idea what Andres was talking about yet again.* "*Either way it sounds like the hatchet will kill me.*"

"Well, mi hija, that would be unfortunate wouldn't it?"
replied Andres with a wink.

The train ride back to Calcutta was generally uneventful,
or perhaps our fear and desperation to get out of the country
had taken over at that point. It was also a journey of angry
silence as my friends clearly held me responsible for
everything that had gone wrong. At one stage the train was
stopped and boarded by police which sent us all into a panic,
convinced we were about to be arrested though I have no
idea what for. As it turned out there had been a murder on
the train. Could this trip get any worse? That's a rhetorical
question. The police came into each compartment asking if
we had seen anything unusual, out of the normal. That was
not an easy question to answer. Since the day we had arrived
in India everything we had seen was unusual and far from
our idea of normality. However I got the impression that the
police were not looking to hear about our travel woes. We
shrugged, said we hadn't seen or heard anything and soon
the train continued on its way. We asked for no details on the
murder nor questioned the likelihood that the murderer(s)
was still on board – somehow it just seemed better not to
know by that point.

Even when the plane finally took off there was still a lump
of fear in my throat that we would be made turn back. As we
waited on the runway, I turned the air conditioner toward me
as the heat was rapidly becoming unbearable. As I did so the
entire compartment that held the light and air switches fell
on top of me. I managed to stop a passing flight attendant
who listened impatiently as I tried to explain what had
happened, then she walked off without a word. A minute or
two later the flight attendant returned and handed me some
duct tape. Clearly this was a DIY flight! That sinking feeling
strengthened in the pit of my stomach as I wondered just how
much of the plane was held together with duct tape. It was
not until touch down in Bangkok that I felt I could breathe

again. We all spent the next few days paralysed in a hotel room with Delhi Belly of varying degrees but grateful to have made it out of Calcutta with our limbs intact.

So you would think that the India experience would have taught me to do my homework before I set foot on foreign soil; get a bit of political, social and geographical insight. Yet less than a year later I was flying into South America blissfully unaware of how my life was about to be turned upside down in ways I could never have imagined.

"You must not run before you can walk." Andres' gentle rebuke reminded me of a time in primary school. My class were taken to the local swimming pool; those who could swim already were told to stand to the left as they would receive diving lessons, those who could not swim would go to the right and have swimming lessons. I could not swim but I watched as my friends and all the 'cool' kids went to the left, so I joined them. All I could think about was the humiliation of admitting I could not swim, not the consequences of how this might affect my ability to learn to dive.

On *my first and only attempt at diving I was terrified, but pride took over. There was no way I was going to show people I was scared. I jumped, pleased by my determination, until I hit the water. While I bounced back up, I realised I was in the deep end of the pool with no way to get to the side and panic set in. My pride abandoned, I began splashing frantically and shouting for help as I sank. The lifeguard jumped in while everyone watched my humiliating fall from grace. As I stood by the side of the pool, still gasping, my teacher shouted loudly at me for my idiocy and pointed for me to join the non-swimmers. I never returned to swimming lessons and I was far into my adult years before I ever learned to swim properly. That day was a painful lesson, although one it took me many years to fully learn from.*

"*Jumping in is not always a bad thing mi hija. It is what brought you to me is it not?*"

"*It never ends well is the lesson I learned.*" I replied cynically.

"*No, you learned always to make sure there's a lifeguard close by when you jump in. That is a wonderful and valuable lesson.*"

VIII

For years I carried around the same packet of Polo Mints. Every so often I would eat one. They travelled everywhere with me. They were, without doubt, the most travelled Polo Mints in the world! I was afraid that if I finished them then everything would be over – the travels, the memories, the people I was trying so desperately to hold on to – that I would be forced to stop. I'm not even sure what 'everything' is. Perhaps the fear is that if I stopped I would have to think about all that has happened. Keeping on the move has kept me busy and sharpened my keen skill of avoidance. I have this dread of everything coming to an end before I've really achieved anything. People frequently talk to me about all the amazing things I have done (in their opinion), all the places I have visited and the incredible things I have attained. All I can think about is what I have failed to do, what I have not yet accomplished. And I constantly feel my time is running out. Am I the only person who thinks like this?

The Polo Mint wrapper was old and torn and the foil inside wrapper left little silver marks on my fingers it was so old. The silver stuck to my fingers and then to the selected Polo Mints that I ate. I noticed they were also becoming a little soft but still I couldn't throw them away. Eventually I knew I would have to eat them despite the unwanted ending I believed this would bring. The easiest thing would have been for me never to eat them, but that would have been cheating. And I am no cheat. A liar perhaps, a thief definitely (for which as I have already explained I blame God and Catholicism) but not a cheat. It would be so much easier if I were. The danger was in knowing the Polo Mints would one day disappear, after all everything always does and there is nothing, absolutely nothing, I nor anyone else can do about it. Sometimes I would even forget they were *that* packet of Polo Mints and I would eat one by mistake and then I would panic. I wasn't ready to let go of them. I wasn't ready for what that would mean.

"Everything is transient in this life."

"Not helpful Andres." Those words were starting to sound like my mantra around Andres.

"We hold onto that which is no longer helpful because it is more comfortable. Sometimes it's a job, a belief, a relationship, a perspective...even a packet of Polo Mints." Andres grinned at me as he continued, *"The truth you believe and cling to makes you unavailable to anything new. You work so hard to hold on to your false truths..."*

"...because sometimes they are all we have?" I offered my response more as a question than with any sense of certainty that I knew what I was talking about.

"Holding on to false truths is about fear. It keeps us static. We can learn nothing from it. We read into it what suits our close-minded view, blind to any truth that deviates from our own. We should not hold on to things that no longer serve us mi hija, whatever those may be." I looked down. His words made sense but I could feel myself resisting them regardless. How much had I held on to over the years that not only had ceased to serve me, but had begun to destroy me in so many ways? Andres continued as if he had been reading my mind, *" What do you hold onto that no longer serves you?"*

I smiled as I looked up, *"A fading packet of Polo Mints."*

Andres smiled back, *"Well that's a start."*

I was thinking about how I used to believe you couldn't really know a country and its people until you had lived there for a time – perhaps a couple of months, a year or longer, long enough to get a true taste of the place behind the superficial gloss of a brief tourist visit. I think it was because I had travelled so much and yet only seemed to see brief glimpses of places as I passed through. Then I started staying in places longer, working and living in those places...and everything changed. Now I would say you don't really know a country until you've had your life threatened there, been imprisoned, beaten, betrayed or had voodoo spells cast upon you. There is something about those things that breeds a sense of familiarity and belonging that you simply do not expect. What does that say about me I wonder?

I told you, that's what I do. I make jokes about everything. And I laugh at them because deep down I believe that I am the only one that has earned the right to find them funny. Over the years I have learned that if you turn everything into a funny story people don't ask too many questions. Feed them just the right amount of information: shock them a little, make them laugh a little - fool them into thinking they know you, then walk away. But the truth is I am the *only* one who has the right to laugh at those things, the *only* one who has the right to cry and mourn what has happened. I have paid my dues. The irony is that the stories I tell are so incredulous people think I am either lying or exaggerating. That makes me laugh, if only they knew that in essence they are watered down versions of the truth; the palatable version for them to digest across the dinner table. They get the edited version, the toned down for public consumption version. And those stories that they say are too incredible to be true... they are my life.

We all create images for ourselves to make our existence that little bit easier to bear. Little white lies that become so frequent and ingrained that we begin to call them our truth and believe our own lies, after all they can be so convincing. Really we only need to convince ourselves. We are always imagining ourselves differently from the harsh and naked reality we spend our life hiding round corners from. The truth is pushed so far to the back of our mind that when it finally returns it has been filtered and tainted to such a degree that it is barely recognisable at times. We call this a sweeter remembrance. So, am I the person I imagine myself to be? Are any of us? Surely the imagined me has an equal claim to reality . . . surely? I hope so because I think I like her more, much more.

Sometimes when I think back to what has happened, I wonder if it is all an elaborate lie. Did I create these stories in my mind and then tell them so often in their various forms that I too have come to believe my own lies? In reality, what if they never happened? What if they are simply a construct of my over-active imagination? Sometimes I wish that were true. It would be so much easier to erase them from my memory if that were the case. And this is the problem, it would be easier yet I know without doubt that if I had to go through it all again, I would make the same choices. What the hell is wrong with me? The only certainty I have is that I would not leave this path even though I do not want to be on it. How crazy is that?

When I was in primary school one year, my parents opened a report card from my teacher and she had commented that I was a pleasant, well-behaved and polite student. She added however that she did have one small complaint, that I had too much imagination. I was a child! Instead of criticising that, they should have been nurturing it. But it was seen as a flaw, a problem to be nipped in the bud. Perhaps report cards in general became a problem for me after that. I could never get it quite right. If I got good grades there would be a criticism of my behaviour; if my behaviour were commended there would be a bad grade in the mix.

Once when I was in high school I remember opening my report card, as usual, before handing it over to my parents. It was a sea of A's for my work and also for behaviour with one small exception. I was thrilled and excited to hand it over to my parents who I assumed would be equally delighted. I rushed home, handed the envelope to my dad exclaiming, "It's all perfect except for one behavioural grade!" It was one grade amid so many, who would care I foolishly thought. My father opened it up and all that followed happened in slow motion. One minute he had been sitting on the sofa, the next I was pinned against the wall as he shouted in my face. He was like a man possessed.

"You got a D!" he hissed at me.

"It was only one, all the others are A's." I replied confused, clearly missing the point.

"You got a D!" he hissed again, "You got a D for behaviour!" He could barely speak, his fury was so extreme, "How could you shame us like this?" Well he certainly seemed to be taking it all a little too personally. Talk about over-reacting! He was waving the report in one hand and holding me against the wall with the other; his face was so red I began to fear he might have a heart attack and I, for some reason that I still could not understand, would be held responsible.

"But I got A's for..." My father's grip tightened and I stopped mid-sentence.

"You got a D! You got a D for behaviour in Religious Studies!" I don't think my father could have been more distraught if he'd been told that I had murdered someone. Okay, I should have realised the subject area might have been a sensitive one, but I honestly (not to mention incredibly stupidly) thought all the A's would outweigh the D, but it was all my father could see. To this day I still don't even know why I got that D. The teacher was never able to control the class and as revenge she gave everyone in the class a D, but I was the only one with parents who actually cared.

Over the next few weeks I learned that my father's fury had no bounds. I was grounded which, as a punishment alone would have been bearable, but he did not stop there. My father wrote a lengthy letter to my Religious Studies teacher profusely apologising for my disgraceful and unacceptable behaviour and asking her to call them direct if my behaviour were less than perfect in the future. He then told me to deliver it! As if! By that stage he couldn't punish me anymore, so I didn't care what he did. I certainly was not delivering that grovelling letter to some crazy woman apologising for something I hadn't even done. It was a matter of principle! As such it was also a battle I thought I could win. I was wrong. My father called my sister and told her to deliver it instead. She did. My sister, I believe, was prompted to do this for two reasons; one was fear of my father and the repercussions refusal might bring; the other was her on-again, off-again hatred for me. Obviously we were going through a 'hate on-again' stage!

As I said before, I'm amazed I made it through high school unscathed. I'm not sure that is an accurate description. I was an outsider, but able to blend into anonymity. I was a nobody. Not known enough to be a part of the popular groups; not known enough to be too much of a target. A threat to no-one.

In the films I create in my mind I am always the winner. Undefeated, I always have the witty one-liners, the enchanting ways, the undoubted upper hand, the strength to deal with any situation. Then again in my mind I'm also a master in all martial arts, wealthy and stunningly beautiful. And in reality? That would depend on it being the immediate reality, or the filtered aftertaste. Who knows anyway? And who really cares? Except I can only be the me in my mind if I solely reside in my mind. Unfortunately the world outside continually interrupts and threatens that existence.

Would I have lived my life differently if I my grandfather had lived? Someone to always worry about the crazy things I do, the unheard of places I land in and the

118

seemingly dangerous situations I always manage to get myself into? I have been wondering about that, wondering if it would have, if it could have, made a difference. In the past I was always so sure it would have. What surprises me most now though is that I don't know the answer. I honestly don't know. All of this is my roundabout attempt to explain (or try to avoid explaining) how I ended up in Arajua. I told you it was neither a short nor simple story. The truth is I have no idea why I went there and even less idea why I stayed.

"Why am I here?" Andres asked, looking at me intently.
"What?"
"This is what you must ask yourself."
"What?"
'Why am I here?"
"Why I am here? Or why are you here?" Andres raised an eyebrow and I could sense a scolding coming my way.
"Why am I here?"
"Andres, repetition isn't helping you know, in fact it's most definitely having the opposite effect. Do you mean me? Why am I here? Right here, right now?"
"Why am I here?" I could have screamed at this point and was ready to kill him if he asked me one more time.
"I don't know why the hell I'm here in this place, today, on this planet. I don't know why I was born. I don't know what my purpose is or if I even have one. I don't know why these things happen to me. I don't know why I have a hole in my head. Hell, I don't even know if I really do have a hole in my head. I don't know why I can't just fit in, blend into non-existence. I don't know what I'm doing...I don't know anything!" I shouted furiously.
Andres interrupted me with a smile, "Finally we're getting somewhere."

IX

Do you know that in the Arajuani language the word for tomorrow doesn't exist? It doesn't exist because tomorrow doesn't exist. When the Arajuani want to say tomorrow, or 'I'll see you tomorrow', they say *ko'ee*. Do you know what that means? If I awake, literally if tonight the world doesn't end then I will see you tomorrow. And when 'tomorrow' doesn't exist provision for tomorrow doesn't exist, preparation for a tomorrow doesn't exist. Everybody lives for the moment and cares little for the future. And that is the destiny of Arajua. It also appears to be my own destiny.

So how did I end up in Arajua? Two months prior to my departure, and my decision to leave, one of my friends had been killed in a freak road accident. It had had a profound effect on me, much to my surprise. I know you may think that sounds callous but I don't mean it that way. I had developed a great immunity to losing people after my grandfather's death. I processed death with a logic that upset anyone and everyone I ever saw fit to share it with. But when my friend was killed many things upset me – how young she was, how random the accident had been, all the things she would never do... all natural thought processes when you lose someone. She was extremely beautiful and I couldn't get the thought out of my head that someone so beautiful could be extinguished so easily; that such beauty had ceased to exist in a fraction of a second and with it every hope, dream, plan for the future she had.

"Our names are written in water." Andres ran his finger over the top of his glass as he spoke. the line his finger made in the water quickly disappeared leaving no trace.

"But it seems so unfair, so random. Do people just forget then?"

"To continue with our lives is not to forget. Death is the destination we all share." Andres paused, deep in thought, *"When people do not tell their stories, they die a slow and lonely death, one small piece at a time. That is why they need a sin eater. That is why they need you."*

"Lucky me." I replied sarcastically.

"Indeed!" responded Andres choosing to ignore my sarcasm.

"You know Andres I don't fear death, but I do fear all that I have not achieved in my life. Everything just feels so temporary. I always feel time is running out to do what I need to do. I don't even know what it is that I need to do."

"Everything feels so temporary because it is mi hija." Andres replied laughing, *"Even our longest days form part of our short time on earth. Our shadows form a boundary and it is rarely clear where one ends and another begins. A sin eater is destined to walk among the shadows, joining them in their hushed conversations."*

"Andres why do you always have to speak in riddles. Can't you simply answer me with a direct, clear response?" My frustration was obvious and I was making no attempt to hide it.

"Well then mi hija you will need to learn to ask clear and direct questions."

"I thought I was!" I snapped back.

"Perhaps your listening is the problem." Andres grinned as I glared back stifling the frustrated scream that was building inside of me, *"Maya we must learn how to die, it is a process. Many fear death but the truth is that a fear of death is more about a fear of living. Everyone dies mi hija, but not everyone lives."*

When my friend died, what I found hardest was the reaction of everyone around me. I could not bear the outpouring of grief, nor the expectancy that everyone, including me, react in this way. We all deal with death differently and I have learned over the years that I do not deal with it the same as those around me. It would be easy to blame Andres what others consider this strange attitude of mine, but the truth is I have always been that way and he is not responsible. So when the idea of going to Arajua came to me somewhat randomly (as do most of my ideas and plans), it was a way to get as much distance between myself and all these grieving people; distance from knowing that in their eyes I would never react the right way nor say the right thing. Truthfully, I just wanted to be anywhere but where I was.

At university I had known some Arajuans and that is where the idea came from I guess. Had I known some Mongolians or Koreans I would probably have ended up in one of those places. There was no rhyme nor reason to it being Arajua. Latin America intrigued me and I loved the Spanish language. My geographical awareness is dubious at best, so I actually had no clear idea where Arajua was. I mean I could tell you it was sandwiched between Argentina and Brazil, and that certainly made me sound quite impressive, however that in itself means little. At that time I would have struggled to tell you where Argentina and Brazil actually were! However my geography has improved over the years, mainly thanks to extensive travels and the need to plan escape routes! When the Arajuans I had known years previously at university had finished their studies and were returning home, they had casually told me that one day I should visit. So one day I decided to do just that. It turns out they were just being polite and didn't ever expect or, I fear, want me to turn up there.

Had I done my homework I would have known that Arajua was fresh out of an almost thirty eight year dictatorship, considered one of the bloodiest and most terrifying in Latin American history. I would have known that the current democratic government was made up of the parliamentary members of the aforementioned dictatorship. Had I done my homework I would also have learned that more than half the country was classified as having third world status and the rest were still living in post-dictatorship fear of what may happen to them if they dared speak their mind. Had I done my homework I would have perhaps reconsidered my choice. I, however, knew none of these things, nor did I care.

In South America anti-communist hysteria and fear took a sinister turn after the Second World War: one that was to affect the lives of all Latin Americans in one form or another. Concepts of freedom were rewritten through a series of dictatorships that sprang up throughout the 1950s. Generations were reared with a new understanding of what political freedom meant; with a new understanding of what freedom meant in general. All countries suffered but Arajua was a unique case in many ways as it was the only one that had no democratic tradition to fall back on, having experienced centuries of turmoil and repression. How do you fight for a return to a period of democracy and freedom, if that time has never existed? What do you aim for with political freedom if you have nothing to compare the current system with? Looking back at their history I guess centuries of oppression created a survival instinct in Arajuans that at times can appear as apathy or non-action, but to view it only as such, is to misjudge the strength of will to survive in a country that has little hope for a better future. Arajua was a difficult country for me to understand and to come to terms with at times, but it fascinated me. Its complex history, its contradictory way of life, the extremes - for everything is an extreme in Arajua - drew me in like a spider which had spun its web to trap its prey. There is an old saying that to get rid of the cobweb you must kill the spider. In Arajua the spiders thrive, and so time and time again many are caught in their webs. And that was to be my fate…for a time at least.

From 1955 to 1993 General Carlos Mendoza ruled the country after a coup d'etat. He ensured his grip on power through political purges, tortures, murders, exiles and bogus elections. He was re-elected seven consecutive times making his rule the longest in 20th-century Latin American history and in the Western hemisphere. He always forcefully denied that he was a dictator and skilfully escaped solid proof of the inhumane crimes committed in his name. Something I learned the hard way when referring to him as a dictator in the company of his many staunch supporters. But why am I telling you this? I'm telling you because so little is known about what happened during his rule. How was it possible that the world knew so little, that so many were never punished for the human rights atrocities that occurred during those years? These questions remain unanswered but these events formed the foundation on which I was to discover, build and hone my abilities as a sin eater. I went to Arajua blissfully ignorant and left painfully aware.

Mendoza's dictatorship was at once effective and selective. Most people were untouched by it personally, if they chose not to question it or get involved in the 'wrong' kind of politics. For many Arajuans, it was a time of security, growth and tranquillity that the present democracy has consistently failed to offer. Those who did question it were effectively and rapidly dealt with. In 1993, Mendoza was overthrown in a military coup. Some things improved but history and corruption have resulted in every successive government being far from any true concept of democracy, not least because so many successive governments have been formed from those who formed part of Mendoza's dictatorship or their descendants. I arrived in the early nineties, just a couple of years after Mendoza had been overthrown. In other words, I arrived in a post-Mendoza era, that is in a relatively post-dictatorship Arajua. The romantic notions I arrived with were replaced over the years with a harsh reality check as victims and torturers alike sought me out as the sin eater who would carry their stories. But that is a story I will come to in time. What you need to know is, for better or worse, this is the country I decided to make my home for almost a decade. Did I say 'decided'? No, I did not decide, nor did I choose. Arajua chose me.

"Serendipity." Andres smiled his annoying smile that always meant he knew something I did not.

"Is that what you call it? Considering all that's happened I'm not sure 'unexpected good luck' is the definition I would describe those years or any that have followed for that matter. Arajua was no easy place to live."

"Is anywhere?" Annoying as Andres' question was, I considered the truth of it thinking I had understood his intention, but then he blindsided me. "It is not easy to live in our own heads wherever our physical body may be."

"Are you suggesting I move out of my own head?" I asked sarcastically, "After all there's a hole in it ready for me to exit."

"An interesting idea. Where would you move to mi hija?" He replied playing with me.

"Anywhere but here." You have no idea how many times I have said those three words in my life. It took so long to realise it was never the physical places I was trying to escape. It was myself; my head, my thoughts. I spent so many years running from the idea of being a sin eater. Years running from the endless people who seemed to chase me so they could tell me their stories. I exhausted myself without realising it. Finally I stopped and, in that moment, realised I had been running from my own shadow and she had been there right behind me every step of the way. When

I stopped it was as if the sun set and she finally joined with me. Finally we moved as one.

"You lack perspective." I snapped back to attention as Andres spoke. He smiled as I groaned, aware I was being taught something but as usual no clear idea what; aware I had missed the point somehow yet again.

"Isn't serendipity just lucky coincidence?"

"Ah you don't like my word, is that the problem? Perhaps you are right and synchronicity would be the better word here. So would you prefer that? Nothing happens to us by chance. "He paused pondering on his own thoughts, "Yes, synchronicity."

"You certainly like the letter 's' today Andres!"

"It is rather a nice letter. A beautiful sound," replied a laughing Andres, repeating the letter 's' in a low hum.

'Great! Let's pick a new letter every day. What fun we could have!"

"Ah mi hija is this you avoiding a difficult topic with that unruly mouth of yours?"

"Unruly mouth?" I replied in disbelief. What a cheek!

"We were discussing synchronicity. Try to stay focused. You have the attention span of a sesame seed."

"A sesame seed!"

"Okay, okay let us not insult the sesame seed and return to our word - synchronicity."

"Are you saying I have no control over my destiny, my fate? That seems a little unfair." I was determined to stay focused despite feeling I had just been insulted or scolded. Probably both.

"It is not what I said."

"So what are you saying?"

"All things happen in perfect timing." Andres paused, "As is your will, so is your deed, so is your destiny."

I dropped my head into my hands exhausted and confused.

X

The couple of years that followed my first encounter with Andres witnessed many drastic changes in my life, though none seemed in any way linked to my experience with the world of mysticism. Moreover I was cynical that the chickens and rooster had actually been listening to anything I said that day and I'm dubious whether they did run off into the countryside with my hopes and dreams. They probably ended up on someone's dinner table later that day as they staggered around bewildered and traumatised from the whole experience. I can't help but wonder, if they did die, did my hopes and dreams die with them? Listen to me! Anyone would think I believed this stuff! Perhaps the link between my encounter with Andres and his magical world seemed implausible at the time, but now I am no longer sure.

I had been teaching theatre for a number of years – never really focusing on my writing nor anything else for that matter. Everything in my life was just a means to an end. And the end was to get through one day in order to make it to the next. Perhaps I should point out it's not that I knew much about theatre: I didn't know a thing; I was just good at bluffing my way into doing almost anything I wasn't desperate to do. I'm also a quick learner when it comes to things I have no interest in learning. It's a gift! Give me something I really want however and I will procrastinate, run and self-destruct at every turn. So I found myself directing large-scale productions with little purpose and even less meaning, but nonetheless they pulled in the crowds and helped me establish a name for myself in theatrical circles. In fact I had managed to establish enough of a name for myself to be hated – always a good sign of success if nothing else! I now know it was that which led to the egun in the first place, and on the path to meet Andres.

Anyway my life was kind of predictable and safe, or so I mistakenly thought. I am speaking in relative terms here. I do know my idea of predictable and safe is a world apart from anyone else's. After my encounter with Andres I had become determined to keep all drama as far from my door as possible, somewhat ironic that I sought to achieve this in the theatre. Not to mention the fact that I was living in South America, in a politically and socially insecure, tumultuous country. But apart from all that, life was predictable and dull. Oh well that is if you don't include the death threats or the endless phone calls with random people telling me in a husky voice to get out of the country 'or else'. Remember, I did mention a lot of people appeared to hate me. Over the years I've noticed that people tend to react to me in extremes of love and hate and not much in between. I think the hate camp definitely has more followers.

Psychologically the phone calls were the worst. It's not that I was actually afraid, but they were incessant. I mean at times you would be putting the phone down and it would ring again and again non-stop, minute after minute, hour after hour, at all hours of the day and night. In the end I got an answering machine and never ever answered my phone until I knew who was ringing. Something I still did when I returned to the UK. To this day I refuse to answer a phone unless I know who is calling. If I don't recognise the number or they don't leave a message I assume it is nobody worth speaking to, or a salesperson (also covered then by 'nobody worth speaking to'). It may also explain why I never win those phone-in competitions on the television that I'm always entering – they've probably called me numerous times over the years to say I've won a fortune and I didn't pick up. That would be typical of my luck. Even now if someone does not speak immediately when I answer

130

the phone, I have an irrational fear that that those incessant phone calls will start all over again. Actually I am terrible at answering my phone and phoning people: I just have a general aversion to the phone. Anyway in the phone calls they would tell me to get out the country; what they thought of me (which was never particularly flattering); that nobody wanted me there (probably true) and that people wanted rid of me one way or another. The latter was accompanied by graphic descriptions of how they planned to do this. The scariest part was that they seemed to know everything about my life and every move I made. Initially my understanding was limited as they often spoke in Arapara – a mix of Spanish and the indigenous language Arajuani which has now become a language in its own right. However I always got the gist of what they wanted to say and as my understanding increased it was clear I had fully understood their intent.

Strangely the calls themselves didn't actually scare me: but at times they did wear me down. I never believed that the things they said they would do to me might actually happen. I guess you need to know Arajua and Arajuans to understand that, before you jump to the conclusion that I am some reckless, thrill-seeking, junky. It is just that they are always threatening to do things, but when it comes down to it nobody acts. Well actually not always but most of the time, and I was convinced this was one such time. The messages moved on to telling me that I was being watched and sure enough, for a long time, I was followed and watched and no secret was made of this. Of course it was all intended to instil great fear – to ensure that I knew whoever it was calling the shots, it certainly wasn't me. It didn't however instil so much fear as it did irritation. And what do you do in a country like Arajua? Go to the police? The concept is ridiculous – the police were more dangerous than the criminals! In fact in most cases the criminals are the police! To convince the police to act usually required a hefty payment and even then there would be no guarantees. I was safer dealing with it alone or, to be more precise, simply not dealing with it and seeing who would tire of the stupid game first. In which case I had the edge, as I had incredible stubbornness and pig-headedness on my side. The police would have refused to help anyway, too much work for something that was too hard to prove and from which there was no money to be gained. Everyone around me was nervous or scared, but I had just reached a point where I couldn't care less about it or anything really. Incidentally that's not bravery, it's apathy – a theme which I fear runs through my life story. The difference is very important. I have been credited with some courageous actions over the years and it makes me so ashamed for the truth is that apathy has been my driving force more often than not, ironic and contradictory as that may sound. Perhaps that's why Arajua was a good match for me: we shared an apathetic bond.

On top of all that there were the personal attacks in the press and on the television by 'celebrities' criticising my work, not that any of them had actually seen it. I should point out that it takes ridiculously little to become a celebrity in Arajua, and celebrity status in such a place is rarely long-lived. After a while I got so sick of it that I used to call them up to confront them and they would never know what to say – confrontation, directness were not the South American approach and they rarely knew what to do about it except avoid me at all costs! But, as they say, all publicity is good publicity – I was known for my theatre work (perhaps renowned would be more apt) and both I, and the groups I worked with, were viewed as a threat. A threat to what, I still have no idea.

There were also the incidents in the theatre – the bomb threats, the sabotaging of the scenery, threats to me personally, including black magic packages. I realise it's somewhat disturbing that I just listed bomb threats as if it were an everyday thing. I would arrive at the theatre each day to find rice thrown across the front pathway and every day I would sweep it up until one day a friend shrieked with horror on seeing me do this. Apparently she was putting it there as part of a protection spell to keep evil at bay, and every day I was removing it, opening the doors and allowing evil spirits and black magic practitioners to enter unobstructed. The way I figured, as I told her, if they were buying a ticket and filling the chairs they were all welcome: good evil, alive or dead, I was no longer fussy!

The first time they (I say they with no idea who 'they' were) sabotaged the scenery was the hardest and then I guess I just learned to accept it, then to expect it and finally simply to live with it. I had costumes and scenery destroyed; I would lose contracts because people were told not to work for me, or they heard rumours about evil spirits in the theatre where I worked: evil spirits that were apparently attracted there by my presence and their desire (along with a few more corporeal spirits) to destroy me. *Everything* was a fight and I just became so so tired of it all. Tired of putting on a face to meet the world. Tired of pretending I wasn't hurt or offended. Tired by the betrayals and the inability to trust people around me. Tired! And still I stayed. It was as if I knew something else were coming and I had to stay there to fulfil it even though I didn't know what *it* was.

"It seems like everything always has to be a fight. It's exhausting." I complained to Andres.

"Stamping your feet and complaining like a child isn't helpful mi hija."

"And neither is that comment." I replied indignantly.

"Everything does not have to be a fight. You are focused on the past or the future so much, you forget how to live in the present."

"The past haunts me and the future beckons, there's very little to keep me focused in the present." I shot back at him angrily.

"Between the past and the future is the here and now. It is there you will find the space for your thoughts."

"You make it sound so easy." I replied disillusioned by such a simple yet impossible task. Giving time to my thoughts, processing all that had happened, was a job I always put off for another day, the tomorrow that never came, the tomorrow I had no intention of allowing to come.

"Learn to balance yourself effortlessly. You cannot change the past; you cannot predict the future. Find peace in the now."

"You ask too much of me Andres. You expect too much of me. You always have." I could no longer hide my disappointment, but I was unsure if it was due to Andres' expectations or my attitude towards myself.

I was so determined not to let 'them' win – many people said I was mad not to just quit and opt for an easier life, that I should have packed up and returned to the UK. Now that is something that anyone who really knows me would never suggest. Maybe they were right, but I objected to people trying to damage what I had worked so hard to build, even if I had built something I didn't actually want. I would have dealt with it a lot better if they had had the courage to show their face but, of course, they never did and I was most definitely and most defiantly not prepared to run from cowards. I am kind of stubborn that way – you know in that cut off your nose to spite your face way as my mother would say. Had I left, my life would have been more straightforward for sure, less tumultuous, safer, friendlier…well when you put it like that even I can't see why I stayed! The thing is that although I've developed running from things into an art form, it has always been on my terms. I made the choice to run each time, so I was definitely not going to let anybody else take that decision away from me. It was one of the few things in my life that I felt I could actually control.

People in the groups I worked with would sometimes leave and some would turn on me no matter what I had done for them; some were sent to join us and would report back about the group, and about me. That hurt, and it hurt that I was watching myself turn into an even more cynical defensive person as time passed. Somehow though that side never won through completely – I've grown up a lot since then and can at least work without the cynicism but with better judgement! I've had to learn to adjust my expectations of others. The backstabbers and betrayers from the theatre group were bad enough without the fact that some of them turned out to have somewhat dubious (are there any other kind?) links to black magic. Actually as I write this – conspiracy theories, black magic, spells and spirits - I can't help laughing to myself about how ridiculous it all must seem. I laugh even more at the thought that this has all now become quite normal for me! When I tell people about some of the things that have happened to me in my life, they laugh and comment on how unbelievable it all seems.

They tell me I should write a book about it and then they laugh and add that of course, as we all know, nobody would ever believe it. And of course they are right. But maybe that is what affords me the protection to tell it – knowing that nobody will ever truly believe me. I am safe – safe in the incredulity of my own life!

The first time I ever received a bomb threat at the theatre was a horrific experience. But after the first time you quickly adapt to it as yet another part of your abnormal normality. It was on opening night and the theatre owners panicked on receiving the anonymous (it would be of course) tip off that a bomb was set to explode just before the start of the play. They called in the bomb squad who arrived in full force – trucks, dogs and all their gear. They proceeded to tear through the theatre leaving confusion and terror everywhere they went. In the end they found nothing, however this did not reassure them at all. As the theatre was an old colonial building with a million nooks and crannies, they stated clearly they could never guarantee to have searched it in its entirety. The bomb squad, in a true Pontius Pilot moment, informed me that it was my decision to empty the building and cancel the performance or, if I chose to go ahead, the life of everyone in the building would become my sole responsibility. They would neither make the decision nor assume any responsibility. I looked at them horrified by the weight of such a decision – not one I had ever, not surprisingly, had to face before. However they did add that if I wanted their opinion, they felt that if it were me potential bombers wanted to get, 'they' would either find a way to destroy the opening performance or, more likely, a way to get directly at me – if 'they' were serious they would succeed one way or another. In other words, they did not think there was a bomb - well, that was my interpretation at any rate. They didn't seem to understand why I didn't feel consoled in any way by their advice. Then they left.

The phone call had said that the bomb was due to go off at eight thirty - thirty minutes before the play was due to begin. The audience would already be arriving and taking their seats or mingling in the café area. First, I decided to keep the public outside without explaining until the last possible moment. I never told the cast anything until afterwards although they were suspicious that something was badly wrong (the bomb squad tearing through the building had of course been a major clue) and some of the girls had, somewhat irritatingly, formed a prayer circle. In between bouts of tears, despite the fact that they didn't know what they were crying about, they called on the Virgin Mary to protect them. I listened to them and groaned inwardly; memories of my parents' fervent devotion to religion stirring in my mind at this most inconvenient time. For some unknown reason, mainly my experience of Arajuan organisational capacity, I was absolutely certain there was no bomb. It was a gamble, an insane gamble, in which I made the decision to risk numerous people's life, including my own. But it was my gamble to take. Ethically it was a somewhat dubious decision, although at the time all I can remember is feeling irritated by the inconvenience of it all. I never stopped to consider the fact that there might actually be a bomb and what might happen as a result. That's me all over, never stopping to consider the consequences of so many of the decisions I make, although the majority usually only put me at risk.

Just before eight thirty I gathered the cast in the auditorium and waited till eight thirty-five before explaining the situation. Some found it funny, most were shocked, and many of the girls wept with a mixture of fear and relief as they began praying again. Then one smart ass pointed out that as everything and everyone was always late in Arajua the bomb would probably go off any minute now. This set nearly everyone off into fits of hysterical laughter; except for the prayer girls who stepped up the frenzy in their devoted pleas to the Lord, the Virgin Mary and anyone else who might have been listening, amid spouting bitter recriminations at me for my recklessness at putting them in danger.

As the public began to enter, we positioned people at the doors to inspect their bags as they came through – without of course explaining why and running the risk of the audience fleeing in fear.

"What are we looking for?" asked one of the 'bag-checkers'.

"A bomb." I replied casually.

"A bomb!" One of them screeched hysterically.

"Calm down or someone might hear you." I hissed back at them.

"There's a bomb?"

"No. Well..yes...well...no...not exactly...well there might be. Look I don't know. Just check people's bags." I replied irritated by the ongoing inconvenience of the whole situation.

"What does a bomb look like?" one of them asked.

"How the hell would I know. Like in the movies I guess."

"Will it be ticking?" came the next question. Oh my God I wanted to kill my bag checkers at this point.

"I DON"T KNOW!"

"What do we do if we find the bomb?"

"It's 'a' bomb, not 'the' bomb." I snarled back. 'The' bomb made it sound so specific and confirmed; 'a' bomb sounded more like a possibility. In my opinion that is.

"Don't make a scene, I don't want people running out of the theatre." At this stage my main concern was still heavily focused on the financial upset if the play were cancelled.

"Will we bring it to you?" I looked at them with a mixture of disbelief and anger. I admit I hadn't thought through the situation, but I knew for sure I didn't want anybody bringing me a bomb whether it was ticking or not. What the hell was I supposed to do with a bomb?

"No! Are you mad?" I then realised it might look bad that they were expected to handle the bomb when I wouldn't, so I quickly added, "I'll be really busy. Just take it outside and put it in a bin then we can call the bomb squad." I'm not sure that's the advice the bomb squad would have given and please know that maturity has opened my eyes to how my behaviour may be interpreted as having been at best unethical.

Unsurprisingly as it turned out the opening went smoothly and there was no bomb. Although considering Arajuan inefficiency there may well have been and it simply failed to explode! Less than a year later both the cast and I were used to regular bomb threats that we ignored with a healthy dismissiveness each time and fortunately our optimistic (some might say reckless) attitude was never tested. The bomb squad and I were on first name terms after a few months, but then they stopped coming when we called and finally we stopped calling. Even the crying girls stopped praying. Everything continued with a calmness one only finds in the eye of a storm.

"When I first came back to talk to you after a few years I was sure you would have forgotten who I was."

"One doesn't forget a head that refuses to close." smiled Andres.

"One tried?" I joked back.

"I told you that you would come back and I told you I would be waiting. I am a man of my word."

"I don't know why I went back. It sounds weird but I missed you. I don't know why, I mean I hardly know you."

"We did share an intense experience." Andres grinned.

"Oh yes. The chickens! Not easy to forget that one!" We both laughed.

"Hard to forget the worst student I ever had." I looked at him with indignation but quickly saw that he had his head down and was chuckling and knew the games were beginning. "I felt I missed something but didn't know what and I thought you might... would know..." I paused, "I knew you would know what it was."

"The student finds the teacher when the time is right. By learning you teach, by teaching you learn. We both needed one another to grow."

"I think you are being a little over generous Andres. What did I bring to the table?"

"Your head." Andres chuckled at the look on my face.

"My head. Great. All I have to offer is a hole in my head."

"Mi hija you still do not appreciate the gift you have been given."

"Gift? You mean curse!"

"Call it what you will. You forget to look at the bigger picture."

"I didn't know there was one."

"You cannot hide the sun with one hand mi hija."

"Yes you can." I mean think about it for a minute, you seriously can.

"I have given you eyes to see the world, why do you keep them closed?"

"I don't like what I see."

"The problem is not what you see, it's..."

"I know, it's my perspective." I completed his sentence with the words I had heard a hundred times. When I first went back to Andres he said he would teach me but I would have to pay. I felt I had my suspicions confirmed and that he was the charlatan I had pegged him for all along. *"And how much will I have to pay?"* I asked him.

"More than you can afford."

"You don't know what I can afford." I retorted angrily, *"Maybe I will teach myself."*

"They say he who undertakes to be his own teacher will have a fool for a student." I sat there trying to work out if Andres had just insulted me, when he stood up saying, *"And that was lesson number one,"* then left the room laughing. As I left his home a boy came up and handed me a piece of paper. On it was written, *"Lesson number 2 – Thursday 9pm. Bring an open mind to go with your open head."*

I had settled into the unreal calm around me, establishing a routine of sorts. And then things changed. An organisation back in the UK asked me to do an article about post dictatorship theatre in Arajua. It seemed a simple enough task. However, even though I lived and worked in Arajuan theatre, I knew very little about it. Actually I knew very little about the dictatorship as a whole. After doing some limited research and asking anyone and everyone I knew for information, I finally wrote the article. But in so doing I had opened up Pandora's box, like the hole in my head, there was to be no closing it from that day forward.

"When Pandora opened the box the trouble began." Andres mused.

"And when you told me my head was open my troubles began."

"That is not true. Your troubles as you call them began when your head opened."

"And when was that?"

"When were you born?" Andres gave me a wry and somewhat ironic smile.

"Great. So basically I've been doomed since birth. Well it never troubled me before you started messing with it."

"That is not true." With Andres I either got short abrupt answers, or lengthy teaching in riddles I never understood. It was infuriating. Then again sometimes he just completely ignored me which was worse. *"Zeus created Pandora as a punishment for mankind. You are an eater of sins to help them."*

"So I'm saving mankind from Zeus' punishment?" I scoffed.

"That is not what I said. When Pandora realised what she had done and tried to close the box, she enclosed 'Hope' inside."

"Is there a point to my Greek mythology lesson?"

"Your open head brings hope, it does not enclose it. The sin eater gives hope by removing a burden from others."

"And giving it all to me!"

"No, mi hija. The sin eater processes the stories. You have the gift to be able to carry them, share what needs to be shared, educate others from the lessons these stories teach."

"I carry their stories into the wind..." I grinned at him.

141

"Exactly." Andres smiled with pleasure at what he assumed to be a glimpse of enlightenment.

"Like the chickens carried mine? Cos I don't think that ended so well Andres."

"You are the most irritating student I have ever worked with..." I laughed at Andres' annoyance, *"...in any of my lifetimes."* But before I could ask what he meant by that he walked out the room, his hand raised behind him to let me know I had to shut up and not try to follow him.

XI

Writing the article on post-dictatorship Arajuan theatre, I began to meet theatre people who worked outside of Coronación – the ones who never got any publicity nor recognition and who used theatre as a social tool – to help the street kids, to make people more aware of the political situation, to help with the incredible poverty that affected so much of the population. An Arajua opened up to me, so different from the one I had been living in. I realised how ignorant I had been about the issues that plagued the country and the history that haunted it. I was exposed to the extreme poverty, the inequality, the corruption and to the many who had survived their brave attempts to challenge almost thirty eight years of dictatorship. I wish I could put the pictures in my head into words, but it's impossible.

I could never make an outsider to Arajua understand this country or these people. They provoke such extremes of love and hate. They will do anything for you, yet so many will also stick a knife in your back at the first opportunity. I mean there are people who reported their own family members to the dictatorial regime of Mendoza. Fear can turn even a loved one into an enemy. Fear can result in a need for self-preservation that devalues any other human life, or any moral standpoint or principle. And anybody who had not been in that position has no right to judge; you never know the choices you will make until you have to make them. That is something Arajua most definitely taught me. You can think you know but until it's tested you cannot say for sure. While the dictatorship brought out the worst in many, it also showed many who had the most incredible will and strength of human spirit. Meeting many of those people taught me what true bravery and heroism is.

In Arajua there is little sense of loyalty as I learned the hard way year after year, perhaps more so because I was a foreigner, the outsider. I am still learning it in all that I do whether that be in Arajua or any other corner of the world in which I find myself. Some lessons, it would seem, are more difficult to learn and retain than others! Something inside of me makes me trust people even when I should know better. I have a need to believe that people will ultimately be good and do the right thing. Ironic I guess coming from the person who stole from Baby Jesus for years! It's a need to believe the possibility that people are ultimately good, although experience has shown me that this is far from the truth. And so every time I would give people another chance, I would try to understand their behaviour, their apathy, because it is too much to accept that these people have such little concept of life outside of their own immediate circle. I tried constantly not to judge people who were always judging me, criticising me, trying to hurt me or my work. People always asked me why I stayed in Arajua for so long, the people I worked with could never understand my decision. So in many ways I am as much of a mystery to the Arajuans as they are to me. At that time, all I knew was that it somehow made sense for me to stay and that when it ceased making sense I knew I would leave.

As I said, I began to learn of another side to Arajua and Arajuans. These new people I met welcomed me, shared with me, trusted me in a way they didn't even trust one another. Then again, Arajuans do not generally seem to trust one another. Perhaps they trusted me more because I was an outsider – I served a purpose for them and when that purpose was complete, we both moved on in our own ways. They shared their stories in detail, they spoke bluntly and directly. That was both an incredible honour and a horrific burden. Working with these people and learning from them was important – I suddenly felt I had a purpose of sorts and my staying in Arajua was starting to make sense.

"*You thought you were interviewing people for an article?*" *Andres laughed*

"*In the beginning I was. But when they started talking they never stopped, they told me about the dictatorship, all that had happened. Their stories went beyond any questions I had asked for the article.*" *The truth is the article was quickly forgotten as I became more steeped in this world of torture and politics.*

"*And your job was to listen and consume. That is the role of the sin eater mi hija.*"

"*I never imagined I would hear such stories. Every time I thought I had heard the worst that one man could do to another, I was wrong. I felt like I was in a daze.*"

"*But you didn't run?*"

"*No.*"

"*You didn't turn your back on them?*"

"*No.*"

"*You didn't refuse to listen?*"

"*No.*"

"*Even when the things they told you brought you pain?*"

"*I stayed.*"

"*Even when the nightmares began?*"

"*I stayed.*"

"*Why mi hija?*"

"*Because I knew I had found my purpose.*"

"*You took their burdens, but in setting them free you also freed yourself.*"

"*Yes.*"

"*But...?*" *Andres had seen the look of doubt on my face and knew I had more to say.*

"*Tell me more about this 'but'.*" *He asked gently.*

"*I think freedom may be over-rated Andres.*"

So much happened in that time. I have little chronological concept of events anymore and sometimes I remember things out of context and laugh at my own madness in doing what I did in staying there. Sometimes I just cry at what I went through, at what I allowed myself to go through. I know if I had a child or a friend who did the same, I would go out and drag them back by the hair if necessary. No that's not true, I probably wouldn't. I could never be that hypocritical, but I would want to. You see in Arajua the good is great, the laughter sincere and contagious, but the bad is soul destroying, insipid with a bleakness and an evil in people that I never imagined I would encounter anywhere but on a cinema screen.

What I know is that we all have moments in our lives that we remember as ones that shape the life we are leading and I was about to have one such moment. Who would have imagined meeting a seventy year old torture survivor and his family could have such a profound effect on me – yet meeting Alberto did and it was to have far reaching effects. My life gained more in perspective and a strange complex friendship united us that was tested to its limits more than once. And although we may not have bounced back from that, our lives are linked, our stories are linked and I will never be able to escape that, if I am to tell this story that I call 'mine'.

Alberto told his story of torture to anyone and everyone who was ever prepared to listen. And that was the issue because nobody ever wanted to listen. This had made him angry and resentful. He talked incessantly trying to get hold of an audience by any means, by relaying any story no matter how banal or how horrific of his torture. He had tried every extreme to be heard and had failed continuously. He had been imprisoned for fifteen years – without charge, without crime. He had been beaten and tortured both psychologically and physically. His hurt and anger were palpable. He needed to be heard and his inability to achieve this terrified him; his fear that he would disappear within his own story and both he and that story would cease to exist.

I don't know why but Alberto chose me to tell his whole story to, every imaginable detail (and some too horrific to be imaginable) of those fifteen years of torture and imprisonment. I will never know why he chose me, but he did. And I will never know why he had to tell so much - the details of every description, some of which I feel were never meant for anyone to hear. He only wanted or needed to express them. I was just a vehicle that somehow made it safe for him to do so. And he hated me for being the one who finally listened. Then he loved me for listening, and then he came to hate me once more as the person who reminded him of the story he had told and not the one he had now rewritten in his head and chose to share with a new audience. I groomed him well and created a monster of sorts – and I left with his story and all that it was to bring upon me.

After Alberto came others, people came to tell me their stories with an expectancy that I could somehow remove them like a surgeon cutting out a cancerous growth. People even began calling me up or approaching me in the street to ask if I was the person they had been told about who would listen to their stories. How do you respond to that? How can you respond to that? 'No' was never a possibility even if at times, so many times, I wished it were. They began to call me the 'Torture Lady' saying I was the one who would always listen to their stories and the one for whom no detail was ever too much. Yet there were times when it was too much - far too much. Is this what it meant to be a sin eater? And so I listened and listened and listened.... I think there is no horror left for me to imagine in this life of one person's cruelty to another, of loss, no form of torture that I have not heard about in every painstaking detail. But their stories were also of how many survived, of how they laughed and how they built their lives again - some better than others. Every time I believed I could take it no more, another would turn up and I would relent. How could I refuse to listen to their pain? So without realising it I became the sin eater as Andres had foretold.

You cannot imagine what it was like to hear these kinds of stories in detail, over and over again. How much can you listen to before it shapes your own life? I have asked myself that so many times because for so long it was my life, and when I went back to the UK and they were no longer there, I was completely lost. Everyone made all these assumptions about what I had been doing in South America, or they just never asked a thing, some just thought of me as some sort of mad socialist or communist who had never quite got that leftist way of thinking out of her system during her university years. A few people kept my sanity at that time, they had all, in some way or another, had a similar experience so we had a common ground to laugh at our own stories and be open about things. It's funny how we somehow gravitate towards the people who are like us, to those who have suffered like us, the ones who can understand without us ever having to explain. Don't get me wrong, I don't for a minute want to go around telling horrific torture stories to anybody who will listen to me. What people don't understand is that the details mean nothing because the stories are about something far deeper and much greater and of course I would love to share that because it is something beautiful and pure.

Everyone saw me as such a serious person, and perhaps they were right. People make their assumptions based on themselves not the other – we don't know how to listen and so we don't know how to hear what is really being said whenever we do listen, how to hear the pleas for help. I made a wild presumption that if I returned to the UK I would automatically fit in because that was where I was from. I was wrong on so many levels. But what I did learn

148

was that once I had time to settle myself, heal myself, others began to find me and the stories continued. It was a new setting, new stories, but the themes remained painfully similar.

"Looking back I don't think I ever fitted in. Even as a child. I think I knew that from that day I chased my shadow all those years ago." I mused sadly.

"Why do you want to fit in?" Andres' question was so simple but I couldn't think of an answer. The truth is anytime I have felt I may be fitting in, I've rebelled against it.

"I want to belong."

"Why?"

"Doesn't everyone?"

"I don't know. I'm not everyone." Andres smiled. *"Fitting in and belonging are not the same thing mi hija. The greatest barrier to belonging is trying to fit in. First you need to learn to belong on the inside. Then you will take that sense of belonging with you wherever you go."*

"I don't understand."

"Fitting in is about how you must change to be accepted by others. Belonging is about being who you are, changing nothing. Belonging speaks of acceptance. Accept who you are mi hija."

"I think that's the hardest thing you've ever asked me to do."

"You constantly seek out confirmation that you don't belong, that you are not enough. Learn to know and respect who you are mi hija, then you will learn what true belonging is."

XII

Sometimes when you are driving and look out the window, up at the sky or out at the countryside, you realise that every place looks much the same. It could be the same sky, the same hills and trees – none of it holds any sense of ownership, of 'belonging'. And I often wonder, if I didn't know where I was, where would I actually be. The only answer I ever seem to find is 'anywhere but here'.

I'm thinking too much once again, trying too hard to form the perfect sentence, the perfect paragraph and thus, the perfect story. Perhaps I'm too uptight – need to loosen up a bit. But I don't think I have ever really known how to do that. It seems I've always been trying so hard to live up to an image I created of myself – but it simply doesn't work like that. Everything always had to be so perfect - perfect strength, perfect beauty, perfect intelligence. And, of course, I always fell short. Never perfect, always defensive, always disappointed. Why, I keep wondering, is the world so much of what I am not? Why does it tempt me with what is always just beyond my grasp or my ability? But this disappointment I mistook for disappointment in life, or rather cynicism of a world structure that failed at every level. The truth was far less dramatic or comforting, it was all simply disappointment in self. Externalising the causes just made it more accommodating. Everything I did was pushed so far to a state of or need for perfection that I inevitably always failed - failed myself.

At this moment, in the silence I now find myself, I have been thinking of the many people in my life, thinking of moments and wondering which, who, what, were the defining ones. But in the end that does not seem as important as being aware that there were defining moments, defining encounters and time passed and those moments last in varied forms because they effected an essential change in the life I was leading and what would lie ahead. I think of stories shared, of my grandparents, of the disappointments, the struggles, the betrayals, the glory, the recognition, the fear, the hate and the love. Right now, most of all, I find myself thinking of Alberto. Meeting him changed the course of my life in ways I could never have foreseen, or perhaps desired. It was a friendship that taught me a great deal about life at its best and its worst; it taught me a great deal about myself and the person I was to become no matter how much I resisted. And so it is, that time and time again, I come to think of Alberto.

"This, what I am about to tell you, about my five thousand four hundred and seventy-six days in prison…has no clear beginning my friend." Alberto spoke with a striking confidence and, at the same time, made no attempt to hide his hostility towards me. Although he called me his friend, he eyed me suspiciously and could never hide the resentment he clearly felt towards me, even though he didn't know me yet. A resentment borne from the belief that he needed me because I was the only one who was prepared to listen. We always sat on the patio of his rundown house when we spoke and drank freshly made mango juice that his wife would prepare and bring in a jug filled with ice. Every chair in the patio was different and each was broken in some way. The view in the distance was of the river, but it was no romantic, scenic view. It was the poor side and the horizon was marked by the makeshift homes of the 'river people'.

"I've become so accustomed to looking back that it is difficult now to disentangle it all; to find a real beginning. And I have to be careful or I may forget how to look forward." Alberto shuffled a little in his chair, crossing and uncrossing his legs. He smiled at me as if we shared a secret, I smiled back with no understanding. "There doesn't seem to be a beginning anymore, my story is just a way of life now. Looking at it from the outside, for someone like you I mean, I guess it all begins the day that you are taken prisoner – especially when you are charged as a political prisoner. You cannot imagine what goes through your mind because you already know all the stories; the disappearances, imprisonment for years without end, the torture, the knowledge that you may lose your life, or even worse, go insane. But it is worse than anything you thought or heard; we would all always have rather died, every one of us. Do you hear me?" Alberto was shouting and pointing at me accusingly, "The truth is that you would welcome it with open arms if only they'd let you. But they don't. No they don't let you." Alberto had raised his voice even further, "They want to see you suffer, suffer and break. You know when the madness is coming, you feel it every moment getting closer, waiting, just waiting for its moment and that, my friend, is what you really fight against every day." I sat there feeling the full force of his words as he lashed out at me in fury. I was guilty of nothing. My only crime was to be the listener.

"At first you tell yourself that it will not last, that it cannot last and you will soon be released. The logical part of you says that they can't hold you for nothing, that they can't just make you disappear from your own life as if it had never even existed. But you know that they can and with such ease that your life seems to have had no value, no worth whatsoever; you might never have existed. Never! Never! Do you hear me? Are you listening? Never! You begin by counting the hours, then the days, then it becomes weeks, months and finally years until the desperation that lingers inside disappears, replaced by the monotonous routine of counting which you continue to do without thought or feeling. It's like counting sheep at night to fall asleep. You finally become so bored of waiting for sleep to come, yet for no reason you continue counting because you've become powerless to do anything else."

All the time he spoke he always seemed to be looking somewhere else, almost distracted by someone or something that I was unable to see. He never looked at me when he was remembering. There were times I thought he was, and then I realised it was a trick of the uneasy yet steady glare from the eye they had blinded during his torture.

"When you've heard so many stories you have already lived the nightmare, you know what to expect and they lose the power to shock you. But you've died a million times over waiting for the moment that they would come and get you." Andres once told me that the fear of what will happen is always greater than the happening itself. I thought about the truth of those words now as I listened to Alberto.

I know the exact date when they took me, the third of March 1964 and the day they set me free, the first of March 1979. At times I begin to make a list of all the things that happened to me during that time because you forget. Can you believe that you actually forget? I think it's a kindness that your own mind does for you amid the tricks it haunts you with at other times and the nightmares that always come back just when you think they've gone forever. But then as I sit alone remembering, thinking about it all, I no longer feel the motivation to remember. Not when I am alone, with others around me it's easier." He looked directly at me. "Do you think that's selfish – to share my nightmare, to pass it on a little? To give it to you?" He chuckled, a private laugh that excluded me. "I don't know. I only know it's easier that way." He stood up and paced a little, as if he had forgotten I was even there and then he rushed back to his chair, leaning forward and staring at me intently.

"I still have nightmares, but not so often anymore. You wake up desperate that you're back there again and it makes

154

you remember that it could happen again. It could! It could happen again!" His voice was rising with a mix of anger and hysteria, "I see when you look at me that you think that's impossible. You think that because you have no real idea. *You* will never know what it was like." He emphasised 'you' to make sure I understood that while he may share his story, he never considered me worthy of hearing it because I had never suffered like him. "And if you knew, if you had seen the evil inside those people, you would believe me that it could happen again. You would know that it *will* happen again." Alberto was shouting at me, his constant defences were exhausting, but he had been doubted and ignored for so long, who could blame him?

"But if they took me again, I'd kill myself. I'd find a way; I don't know how but I would. I have nothing to prove," he added angrily, "You don't believe me, do you? But I would. I'd kill myself. I did my years and I survived. Don't you see? That's how I know I could never do it again." He continued staring at me, defying me to question or doubt him. I stared back but said nothing.

"Like I said, you think you will never forget, that it would be impossible. But you don't realise it's happening, that the memories are changing...with time and distance they somehow just don't seem so bad anymore. Then when you do remember it's as if it all happened to someone else, in a faraway time and another place." He paused, "I wish it had happened to someone else." I looked up, surprised by his admission, but also aware I had heard his voice breaking. I noticed his eyes were full and I quickly looked away worried I would embarrass him.

When Alberto began to tell his story it was impossible to stop him. He never realised how hard it was to listen, hour after hour, as he remembered relentlessly. This was not my reality; this was not a world I ever wanted to recognise. But he left me no choice. I often think, since my return, how impossible it is to share my experiences in a way that people would understand. When I have tried, their blank faces infuriate me. They ask what it was like, but I can see in their eyes that they don't really want to know. They want some neatly summarised version that will entertain them and, most importantly, they want brevity; not stories that make their illusion of safety a little less comfortable. They cannot see that my stories are not negative or of people without hope, for me they tell of love, endurance and strength, of heroism. I have learned not even to try to tell these stories anymore, to allow people their safety in ignorance. I have learned to be silent. Alberto taught me well.

"The sin eater must learn what can be shared and in what form. It is not an easy lesson."

"A bit late telling me that now Andres."

"Would you have listened if I had tried before?"

"Probably not." I admitted reluctantly. Why do I always have to learn the hard way? And why do I always feel defeated by my own inability to learn the easier way.

"That is how we grow mi hija."

"But isn't there a simpler way? Surely there's a simpler way?"

"Your mistakes help you learn who you are not. They teach you about your moral compass."

"What if I don't have a moral compass?" I teased.

"You would not be a sin eater if you had no moral compass," Andres replied unimpressed by my attempt at humour.

"But I've done thing, things you don't know..."

"I see everything."

"No you don't." I snapped back, irritated by Andres' claim to omniscience.

"Maya, do you think stealing from your Baby Jesus means you have no moral compass." I nearly choked as Andres sat there chuckling. How could he possibly know

156

about that? Before I could ask Andres continued still laughing, "I told you I see everything." I stared at him unsure whether to be shocked, suspicious or scared. In the end I had no energy to be anything but resigned to the fact that Andres would always be a step ahead of me. I wasn't trying to compete, I was simply tired of feeling I was constantly running to catch up and every time I thought I had I was sorely mistaken.

"My mother died in 1953 and most of my family were in Bolivia; some hadn't been able to return to Arajua since the revolution in 1943 and others, afterwards, were wanted by Mendoza's government. Wanted for having an individual, creative idea, for expressing an opinion that differed from the one we were told to have! Do you hear me? Are you listening?" Alberto instantly checked I was paying attention, always aggressively, ready to accuse me of failing him if he caught me out. It infuriated me, but then I tried to imagine what it must feel like to carry a story for so long with nobody willing to listen. "My older brother was taken prisoner the year before he died. Luckily, so to speak, they only kept him a year and when he was released he escaped to Bolivia. I never saw him again. They took me in 1964. Have I told you that already?"

Alberto would jump from one story to another, laughing and crying at the things he remembered, oblivious to my presence. I never spoke at those moments; what would I have said? But the silence we shared became an understood one, a recognition of the uselessness of words. Sometimes he would repeat stories over and over. He would ask if he had already told me about it, but never waited for my response before he continued. Whether I said I had heard it already or not, he would tell each story as many times as he needed to in his attempt to find some form of release. Sometimes he would stop in the middle of a sentence and I knew from the look on his face that the memory he had been

157

sharing had triggered another he wanted to forget. And it scared me that in his eyes I could see far worse had happened than the horrors he shared with me. I had no imagination left to guess what they might be.

"What I'm trying to tell you is that I come from a family who always fought against the system and I, we, paid for that. I think I was telling you that my father was killed. I received the news that he disappeared during the first days of 1965. A short time after, my brother Pablo disappeared. We never heard what happened to them but we know they were killed, even now we wait for news; if you don't have a body you can't bury your dead, you can't bury the hope that they might be alive even when you know they are not. The mind, my friend, is always playing tricks on us. You spend every day of your life nourishing the hope, the belief that they might be alive. And soon that hope starts to destroy you; it dictates how you live your life. They know that and that's why they do it. All we knew was that they had disappeared in Chile. My brother was on his way to work, my father was coming to visit me. That was the stupid thing: he knew they were looking for him, but I was his son and he knew better than anyone what they would be doing to me in prison." Alberto spoke with such pride about his father's sacrifice and it was almost as if he cared more about the act than the person who had done it. "He knew because they had done it to him. I think it was the destiny of my family to be prisoners. No, to tell you the truth I don't believe much in destiny; it's just that prison seems to have been a part of my life since I was a child." He stopped at times and I would breathe a sigh of relief, thinking he had finished for the day, but after a time he always continued. I learned to wait silently and never leave until he gave me permission to do so.

"I used to believe in God, a long time ago. Now I don't. How can I believe in the God they told us about as children, the one we stood in church and prayed to? That God

158

abandoned me a long time ago. But I believe in other things - in nature, in the sky and the earth, in the god inside of us. I believe in many things but I do not believe in Him." His defiance betrayed him and I realised the hurt was greater, the need to understand was greater because of his belief in God. I knew it because I felt it too. Don't they say that the closest to an atheist is the true believer? I grew up surrounded by believers, I know one when I meet one, Alberto was a believer.

"So, they arrested me on the third of March. Did I tell you that? They came to my home at dawn and they took my wife and me. We had only been married for two months. We had no children. At times I thought we never would. In prison I thought of that often, of the loss of the children I might never have." Often he would repeat dates, names even particular stories over and over again, with a kind of pride in his own ability to remember, or perhaps disappointment in his inability to forget. "They broke down the door and entered the house with guns and knives and handcuffed me before we even realised what was happening. Can you imagine the fear we felt for each other, the fear we felt for ourselves? That does not make me a coward. Don't you dare think I'm a coward. I'm no coward. Do you hear me? You know they will come for you one day; you live your life expecting it. Isn't it strange how it still comes as such a surprise then when it actually happens?" Alberto would ask a question and look at me but it was clear he did not want an answer, so I never gave him one.

"They put me in the famous 'camioneta roja', the red truck that terrified everyone for almost thirty-eight years. They would drive around the city, slowly, like those vans that look for stray dogs, and people would run. I was the stray they caught that night. I still wanted to believe, needed to believe, that my fate would be different from my brother's and my father's. It was. It was worse. You see,

159

they let me live." And he cried, sobbed without a break for what felt like an eternity. Then as suddenly as he had begun sobbing, he stopped and continued with his story as if nothing had happened. I've witnessed that with many who share their stories with me and it catches me off guard every time. I watch them sob, unsure what to do, unsure if I should speak or comfort them. Some sob with a force that is so painful to watch and hear that it breaks your heart. I have learned to look down and wait. I neither speak nor move. Simply I give them their time to come to terms with their pain. It is such a private moment that nobody is ever intended to see or be a part of…unless you are the sin eater.

"They took me to 'Investigations': my wife also. They kept her there for one year. That was her punishment for having married me." Whenever he made comments like this he would smile wryly and wink at me. I never knew whether to smile back or look away. It was part of his game and I didn't know the rules. "Later she told me she had been pregnant with our first child. They beat her in the stomach until she bled and lost the baby." I wanted to ask more about her, what they had done to her, but I didn't. I knew there were things he would never share with me, things he would never have to. "They kept me there for six months before moving me to a new cell. In those six months things happened to me, terrible things. They tortured me, they put me in the 'pileta', they gave me electric shocks with a cattle prod, they even made me dig my own grave." He shuddered as he remembered. "I don't know where it was exactly, near the river somewhere, and they made me lie in it. Are you listening to me? Just after it got dark they took me, supposedly, to identify the place where I had had secret meetings with other subordinates. I had never been to such meetings. How could I give them information I didn't have" Alberto paused before adding defensively, "I would never have given them any information. They could have killed me and I would have stayed silent. Do you hear me? I never betrayed anyone. Others did, but I didn't. Don't you ever forget that!" He paused to collect himself from his angry outburst and then continued with his story, "When we got to the place they told me to start digging. I didn't realise at first that I was digging my own grave – I assumed it was for someone else, but then they made me lie in it and started to shovel the earth back on top of me." Alberto had begun to sweat and was pacing as he spoke, darting back to the table where I was sitting every so often to ensure I was listening. "And you know I felt absolutely no fear in that moment because I thought if this was the time for it to end, then I was ready: ready and willing to accept an end to all of it. That was how my life was destined to end I thought."

"As I lay there I reached out one hand and laid it outside of the grave. It was shallow enough. They started to pour the earth on me, on my chest, on my legs and they were hitting me with the butt of their rifles, hitting me all over. The pain was so intense but I didn't try to protect myself because I needed to keep my hand outside the grave. I thought if they are going to bury me alive, if they are going to kill me now, then I must keep my hand outside the grave. Then one put the rifle in my mouth and laughing shouted 'You're going to die here you filthy communist!' My teeth were chattering against the rifle. I remember hearing that and being surprised at the fear I didn't know I was even feeling. But all the time I kept my hand outside the grave. I had to. I thought that if they bury me alive someone will see my hand and know that a body is buried here. Someone would tell my wife and my family. They wouldn't have to live with me as 'a disappeared one'."

I had heard so many stories about the 'desaparecidos' (the disappeared ones), about the agony of the families left searching for bodies that were never found. The 'disappeared' were kidnapped or arrested without charge, tortured and murdered. Many were taken from their homes in the middle of the night, tortured at clandestine detention centres and then disposed of. They were killed in an attempt by the junta to silence any social and political opposition and finally their bodies were disappeared by the military. The disappearances left a deep scar on Arajuan society for decades. Their families could never find closure: never find peace.

"But it didn't happen. They buried me up to my neck and then waited a while before pulling me out again while they laughed. They forced me to my knees with their rifles and told me to beg for forgiveness. Maybe because I had thought that this time they were truly going to kill me, I don't know but I think I felt almost emboldened. I didn't care anymore what they did to me. That was their mistake. I felt so angry and thought why should I beg forgiveness for something I haven't done? Why? And I screamed at them that I would not. In my head it seemed like I had screamed those words, but it came out so quietly and so calmly. Of course they heard and well, the beating came like never before, punch after punch, kick after kick until they grew tired of their games and brought me back to Investigations and continued to torture me there." I sensed Alberto's pride in refusing to bend to their will, in his ability to withstand their beatings. He wanted me to know that he was no coward. It was important to him I knew this and he would repeatedly tell me how he had never been broken, how he had never betrayed his friends.

"They brought me back to the 'pileta'. My friend let me tell you about the 'pileta' – the famous 'pileta' that you must have heard so much about. They had many forms of torture, they did many things to us, but what we feared the most was the 'pileta'. It was a bath, a normal one like what you would have at home and fill with water. Only this one was filled with urine, vomit, blood and excrement, all mixed in with the water. The smell alone would have made you sick. They would strip you naked. It was worse if they left you dressed: it added to the indignity because the smell would cling to your clothes, making you sick for days afterwards. Then they would strap your feet to the ground and tie your arms behind your back. One of them would straddle your knees to hold you in position and make it harder to squirm or get up, another would stand on your feet. When they were all positioned another would pull you back by the neck."

"Ask yourself how long you think you could hold your breath. We all always tried to calculate that while we waited in the cells. We knew sooner or later they'd take us to the pileta so we'd practise. But it was in vain. At first you'd try to hold your breath. You'd fool yourself into thinking you could do it. Then at that moment they would punch you in the groin or the stomach so you would gasp in pain and open your mouth. You'd forget you had to keep your mouth closed as the pain shot through your body and in that moment it would all pour into your mouth – excrement from those who had been there before you and your own, the urine, the vomit, everything. You'd remember and try to spit it out, struggling and the more you struggled, the more you gasped...and the more you gasped, the more it poured into your mouth. Soon it was coming in your ears and up your nose, everywhere, and you were gulping it down trying to find air. They would hold you there until you were almost lifeless and then pull you out. Just as you finally caught your breath, once again they would push you back under."

Suddenly he would jump up, excited to show me in detail how they positioned him, how they hurt him. He would act it out, adding to the horror of his words. Then he would become aware of himself, the way we sometimes do with our own laughter – we hear it aloud and stop self-consciously. He would be silent but only for a moment. There was too much to be told and I had been chosen to listen.

"They would do this repeatedly until it seemed that your body could take no more. How we longed for death at those times, longed for them to finally just drown us. They never did. They would unchain us and leave us almost lifeless on the floor while a doctor came to check on us. A doctor who wouldn't know who you were and would never remember your face again. We would remember them. Oh yes, we would remember them, their faces stayed with us for the rest of our lives. They would take our pulse, check our blood pressure and if you were truly damned they'd tell them to wait and let you rest a short while but that then they could continue. What they meant was you weren't going to die yet and your body could withstand more torture. Meanwhile another was put in the 'pileta'. They never wasted any time. Those doctors – they were the ones I hated most, the ones I feared most. They were checking us to see whether our heart could sustain more torture or whether they should stop for the day in case we died on them. They didn't care what happened to us. What kind of doctor does that?" It was another question that required no answer, but Alberto's questions over the days became less angry and more pleading. It was as if he was caught in a never-ending loop of trying to make sense of an evil that had no logic. "If we died then the torture had failed. They knew we would be seen as martyrs by people. You know torture is never about killing people, it's about taking them to the brink and breaking them. They wanted to break us and then send us back to our community as a warning to others. It was their way to say, 'look what happens if you dare to go against our regime'. And for many it worked."

"They didn't want us to die, that was not control, but they wanted to take us as close as possible and pull us back in the final seconds when we most wanted to reach out and embrace death with what little strength we had left and they expected gratitude. The craziest thing of all is that you would feel gratitude. You were grateful to this torturer for

164

stopping! By that time you would tell them anything they wanted to hear, you would betray your friends, even your own family in desperation to have them stop, you would confess to crimes you had never committed. But I never did. I never told them anything." He looked at me out of the corner of his eye, as if to check if I was believing his words, "I'm not trying to say I was brave. I'm not saying that. But I never gave them anything, no matter how much they tortured me. I never betrayed anyone. I never confessed to things I hadn't done. I was able to stay quiet, not because I was brave, no that is not why... it was because I kept thinking if they are going to kill me like this, why should I give them that pleasure. Why? I wasn't brave. No I wasn't brave. But I was angry. I was angry with a fury you could never imagine. But the worst wasn't to be taken to the 'pileta'," I jumped as Alberto began punching the side of his head as if he wanted to punch a memory out of his consciousness, "the worst was to hear the screams of the others already there". He walked to the side of the house and slid down the wall sobbing. After a few minutes he curled into a foetal position, his hands covering his ears as he rocked back and forth. I watched motionless, helpless to alleviate his pain.

I thought I understood Alberto's world, but how could I? Yet he changed mine forever. Like him, I became enclosed in a wall of silence, knowing that I could never share what I had heard, the horrors he had told me. How could I pass that on to another? It had changed me and that was irreversible, but at the same time I knew I had been fortunate, that I had experienced a moment in time in the hours I spent with Alberto that was worth more than even I was capable of understanding. Over the years I began to understand what Andres had taught me: as a sin eater I would learn how to filter the stories. But those parts that I cannot share tell me, what do I do with those?

When I first met Alberto he listed every injury he had received, like a shopping list. I didn't understand then that in a way the physical damage meant precious little to him. "Apart from the beatings, the constant beatings, I lost the sight in one eye because they put an electric cattle prod in it, they burst my eardrum and I am deaf in one ear because they would put a fire hose on just inches away from our heads, they pulled out my teeth, I lost a testicle from the beatings, they say both my kneecaps will need replaced or my legs amputated later because of the damage they did when they would repeatedly beat my knees with metal rods, I have scars all over . . ." On and on the list went perfunctorily. I sat there shocked more by Alberto than by what they had done to him. I didn't know how I was supposed to process this. I didn't know what to say, how to comfort him. But he needed neither my words nor my comfort. And his strength denied pity.

I remember one of the times I became overwhelmed by the tragedy of Alberto's story and telling him he deserved so much more. I felt so useless to help him and so frustrated by my own inabilities to make a difference. I felt so guilty that I had been spared that kind of life and yet part of me envied him in a way that I am unable to explain. We do not know what we are made of until we are tested, but to be tested is a risk. We may not be forged from the mettle we believe or hope we have been. "That's not for me to say, my friend. Others will decide that, through what you write others will judge me. You will write my story. You will tell others. The fact that you are here, giving me your time, listening to what I have to say, that is my job done." He smiled at me, "I don't have the opportunities to bring my story to others, I'll let you do that for me. I have known many people and I have seen great amounts of suffering, far worse than my own. There are things to be written about, my friend, things that would fill a thousand books. I would love to be able to communicate with many people, I have so many things to tell them – I still have my dreams. You will help me realise those dreams." When he said those words I felt so sad and at the same time angry at him, angered and terrified at the weight of the responsibility that he had passed on to me. But it was no different from the weight Andres had passed to me, or the weight I placed on myself.

"Sometimes I have nightmares and in my own dream I say to myself 'Alberto, you're dreaming' and I try with all my strength to make myself wake up. I desperately want to wake up and I've even hit the wall in my sleep trying to force myself to wake. But even that seems to be a part of the dream. Then I say to myself, it's okay Alberto, open the door and go into the cell. I enter and all the others are there. They come to embrace me, my companions from that time. Later I think about how life plays these games with us. What did I do to deserve that life plays with me like that? But it's complicated – it is all so so difficult. I'm sure that people who commit suicide are trying to stop themselves from thinking about that question – what did I do to deserve this? There are times I think about suicide but I don't know if that is in my dreams or when I am awake. It's difficult to know that sometimes. Reality is all mixed up with my dreams. All I want is to sleep: sleep without interruption."

"So many times they said they would set us free but then they never did. So many times I dreamt of that day that I could see it all so clearly. When it happened I felt I was inside my dream and none of it was real. I waited to wake up but I never did. I'm still waiting." He laughed at his private joke that he knew I could not understand. "When they freed me, I went to the parliament building and sat in the plaza outside. And I began to laugh and I laughed and I laughed so loudly until the guard came and told me to move on, that I was not allowed to sit there. Well, everyone has their job to do I guess and he was just doing his. Suddenly I felt as if I didn't know where I was, everything seemed so strange. I felt lost and scared and for a moment wanted to be back in my cell with all that was familiar. Then I heard the cathedral bells ring out five times and I knew that it was five o'clock in the afternoon in Coronación and I was free. But I didn't know what it meant to be free anymore. I didn't know what freedom was anymore. I didn't know where to go or what to do." I guess after fifteen years of imprisonment the outside world can seem more like a prison. Alberto was physically free but the betrayal, the lies, the corruption had imprisoned his mind forever.

"When I went into prison there was no television yet in Arajua, there were no traffic lights. Can you believe that? In fact there were hardly any cars. When I got out, I couldn't even cross the street anymore there were so many cars, I was almost killed trying to cross the road. Can you believe that? Fifteen years of prison and torture to be killed crossing the road! The irony of it. That would have made a great story." We both laughed, "You know, I never felt a prisoner until the day they set me free. It was only then I began to see death, everywhere I looked, even in the eyes of children. Can you imagine anything so awful? All I see is death everywhere I look."

As I tell Alberto's story I wonder now if it is his or mine that is on these pages. Somehow they seem to be inextricably linked. I doubt mine would exist now without him and his would not continue without me. It both amazes and terrifies me to think that our stories have become one forever.

Alberto was found dead on twenty-sixth of February 1994. He had slit his wrists with a rusty razor. He had been free five thousand four hundred and seventy-six days. . . almost fifteen years.

So now as I look out of the car window I see the trees and the sky, there's a certain atmosphere, a certain view and as darkness comes there's something familiar about it all. Buildings have a familiar air, an air that has a familiar

168

colour and smell. And there is a reflection coming from the sea, from the invisible colours on the horizon. In Coronación that line is the greenish blue mist of the Chaco and here it is the greenish blue mist of the ocean. In the end they are all one and the same. In the end our stories follow us wherever we go.

"You are not responsible for his death mi hija."
"Then why does it feel that way?"
"Your job is not to save people, you cannot save them from themselves."
"But surely, if I did my job right, he wouldn't have... I keep asking myself what I could have done"
"You took his story and that is your role. What he chose to do with his life was his decision, his choice, his right."
"But what was the point?"
"Sleep without interruption." Andres echoed the words Alberto has said to me, *"He didn't kill himself because he wanted to die..."*
"Then why?"
"To stop the pain. This world is too much for some people."
"There are so many things I still wanted to say to Alberto. Maybe I could have saved him, stopped him I mean."
"Such arrogance mi hija!?" I looked up at Andres smarting from his comment. I wasn't sure if I was hurt or angry. How dare he call me arrogant? Was he right? Am I so self-consumed? *"Can't you see his name was written in water. You played your role and he played his."*
"But I still feel like I failed him Andres."
"Then mi hija you must greet failure as you pass it on your path, not stop and set up home with it."
"I hate your stupid sayings."
"That is a lie. If you want me to believe your lies you should try at least to wrap them in truth."

"Be careful Andres some liars tell the truth." I grinned at him, feeling I had somehow won but, as always, I was wrong.

"Yes mi hija. It is inevitable that someone who talks a lot will sometimes be right."

XIII

In Arajua the more research I did, the more imbued I became with the horrors of all that had happened. I spent days on end at the Horror Archives. These are archives open to the public that contain details of the dictatorship – orders, arrests, secret reports, death lists and on and on it goes: records that I have been told are second only to those that survived about Nazi Germany. Yet in Arajua the willingness with which members of the public go to these archives is limited at best. Some are afraid to be seen to be digging up the past; others are afraid of what they might find. Even if someone has been missing for years on end and are undoubtedly dead, there remains a hope, a small belief that they may be alive somewhere if you have no body and no papers to state otherwise. For some, I guess, it is actually better not to know, better never to have that final confirmation that removes all hope. So there I sat going through records of imprisonment and torture to try to find any that were relevant to my work. It was horrific, but reading those documents was far easier than listening to the stories; easier than looking at the pain in people's faces as they recalled all they had been through. There is little I don't know about every method of torture that Mendoza's regime used. I know more than anyone should know about such things, and that kind of knowledge never ever leaves you.

When I tried to talk to people about the things I was learning I was met, on the whole, with disinterest. It seemed nobody wanted to remember the past, the present was unbearable and so everyone firmly fixed their gaze on some imagined point of utopia in the future, ignoring all else. Nobody wanted to admit the past and the hideous truth that accompanied it. No one wanted to learn the lessons of the past. I represented the one who would not let go, constantly picking at a scab everyone else wanted to pay no attention to. This did not help my already waning popularity. It also quickly shrank my friendship group.

"Why do we never discuss politics?" I asked Andres.

"Politics were never relevant to either of our journeys. The people were."

"But aren't they intertwined?" After all the dictatorship repressed the people and created the situations and stories I inherited as a sin eater. How could they possibly be separated?

"Politics is the art of looking for possible trouble and, when none is found, creating it, and then convincing people that you have the only solution. Politicians talk; in our work we listen. Never forget that."

"But..."

"When you involve yourself in the politics, how can you be there to listen to the stories of those who have suffered? You will be too preoccupied with matters that do not concern you. And, more importantly, you will have taken sides. The sin eater cannot judge the storyteller or the story ever."

"But... doesn't that mean...?" I looked at Andres aghast as the full realisation of what he was saying dawned on me.

"Yes it does. You do not choose who comes to you. Whether they have been sinned against or are the sinner you must listen and accept their stories without judgement."

"But..." I felt both angry and confused. "Why should I listen to them after what they have done? You're telling me I will have to listen to the torturers? That's not fair!"

"Fair?" Andres had raised his voice and I could hear his anger rising with it for the first time since I had known him. "Who are you to judge? How dare you decide who is

worthy of sharing their stories." I looked down, feeling a mix of both anger and shame. I couldn't get my head around what Andres was saying.

"But Andres...." I pleaded.

"But...but...but..." Andres shouted at me, standing up and pacing. I didn't know what to do except sit and bear his anger. "In all bad we can find good, in all good we can find bad. We do not judge."

"But surely some people are just evil?"

"Mi hija," Andres returned to his seat, his voice now calm, "whoever seeks you out you must listen. If a person is solely evil they would not seek a sin eater to unburden themselves. Can't you see that? Those who seek you need your help. You relieve them of the burden of being themselves. And as you are a part of their salvation, they form a part of yours. That is why the sin eater walks in the shadows."

"Again with the shadows Andres?"

" Without light there can be no shadow mi hija, and we all cast a shadow. Whether we are good or bad, we all cast a shadow."

"Are you saying there is darkness in all of us?"

"Darkness and light co-exist. It is the way of the universe. It is our shadows that connect us. It is our shadows that bring us to the sin eater."

I left Andres' home that day exhausted, uncertain if I could carry this burden, uncertain if I even wanted to. Andres always said our destiny never leads us to paths we cannot manage, no matter how difficult they may seem. But this seemed too much, a step too far. He was right however, as always.

I'd be a liar if I said I came out of it all unscathed. Of course things played on my mind. Of course I had times when I felt the knowledge was all too much, the fear was too much, nights when I cried myself to sleep. But time is a healer, not a great one as the saying goes, simply a healer in that it gives us space to adjust. That is all we do, adjust. Time also acts as a filter to help us remember the better moments and push others into the background. I did have some wonderful moments and met such amazing people during my time in Arajua. Sometimes though I remember the other memories. When I least expect it they come back to me, creeping up from behind. They always manage to find me unprepared and unsuspecting.

Democracy (and I use that term very loosely) had brought new problems for Arajua partly because no one was quite clear or certain about the foundations on which a democracy could and should be built. As I said before, Arajua had never truly lived as a democracy. Its borders had been closed to outside influence for so long through most of its history, that democratic concepts were vague and confused, outweighed by a desire for personal advancement and wealth for many. It became an open invitation to corruption at levels more difficult to achieve under a dictatorship: a dictatorship that had sought primarily to maintain its own privileges and wealthy position and that of those who could most greatly assist it. Workers' uprisings and strikes that handicapped the country for days on end and damaged the already fluctuating economy, replaced censorship and imprisonment. Class divisions became more marked than before as capitalism was embraced by all who could do so: in the process the rich got richer while the poor got poorer. Slowly but surely, for the first time, a growing middle class established itself and levelled a new threat against the status quo. In the midst of all this many mourned the passing of the dictatorship and nostalgically yearned for its speedy return.

These were all things I had never had to consider before, things that had never been part of my existence, or that I had never been forced to question. It made me realise how much I took for granted in my life up to that moment. The large number of nation-wide strikes which occurred began an economic downward spiral culminating in extensive bankruptcies and the collapse of numerous national banks and financial institutions. In the last few months of 2001 violence increased with multiple drive-by shootings and grenade attacks. On the 23rd November 2001 these disturbances came to a head with the assassination of the vice president. The assassination provoked a unanimous reaction in almost all social and political sectors. A series of demonstrations began less than a week after the assassination, in front of the parliament, in an open show of support for the impeachment of the president. This is where I have to rewind a little, as inadvertently and quite incredibly I was dragged into the whole assassination fiasco that occurred. How, you may ask, is that possible? Well, please allow me to attempt to explain the inexplicable.

As a foreigner living and working in the country I needed certain documents including an identity card. The process to obtain this is far from simple and involves obtaining paperwork from multiple offices, paying a lot of people and waiting in interminable queues. This in itself has become a business whereby you pay someone to do all the leg work, collect all the paperwork, wait in all the queues and bring you all you need at the end. These people have contacts enabling them to get things done quicker and easier and for this you pay an extra cost. I had found one such person. Let's call him Mr.X (partly due to a lack of imagination, partly out of fear of repercussions, but mostly because I can't actually remember his name). The process began well. However after a few weeks Mr.X requested more money, claiming he had hit some unforeseen hitches (yeh, like having to pay his own bills). These requests became more frequent and more threatening so I decided enough was enough and I would cut my losses, disengage his services and request that all my paperwork be returned.

In my head that played out as a reasonable and simple plan of action. Only in my head.

I made my request and, to be fair, he accepted the news rather well. Or so I thought. He arranged to drop off all my paperwork that he had completed to date later that morning. Around eleven the doorbell rang and I opened the door to find Mr.X holding a gun in one hand, pointed squarely in my direction, and my papers in a folder in the other. Now at this point in my retelling of the story, many people ask me in horror "What did you do?". It is a question I find bizarre. I mean, I did what anybody would logically do. I grabbed the folder, slammed the door and hid behind the wall (just in case he decided to shoot through the door. Strangely when I say this most people look at me as if I'm mad. It was a risk, I do get that. I'd love to tell you it was a calculated risk but the truth is I just wanted my papers back. It never registered that he might actually shoot me.

After closing the door and sinking to the floor at the side of the wall, a flurry of thoughts and possible scenarios came into my head and none were good. I waited, listening, wondering if he would shoot down the door. He rang the bell incessantly and I stayed motionless out of sight and, hopefully, out of bullet range. You know before I set foot in Arajua I had never even seen a gun close up before. In the years I spent in that country I've lost count of how many times I've now had a gun pointed at me. In fact, it happened so often it became non-threatening which, trust me, is a very unwise and false sense of security to allow yourself to have. Anyway Mr.X left after shouting some things through the door, none of which came across as very complimentary. I also thought I heard something about revenge but I chose to ignore that. What could he possibly do I thought, clearly forgetting where I was living. My experiences with Andres, I think, had emboldened me, or rather fooled me, into thinking I was untouchable. The crazy thing is I know I'm not, but even now I still behave in that somewhat reckless manner.

"You never learn." Andres sighed.

"Okay, okay, I don't need you to keep going on about it." I knew Andres was right, but the stubborn streak in me ensured if he said black, I'd say white whether I thought that or not.

"Stubbornness can be used in a positive way, if only you took the time to learn." Andres' response made me feel that he was in my head once again, reading my thoughts. "How much harm have you caused yourself because of that stubbornness?"

"Is that a rhetorical question?" I knew it was but Andres had pressed my buttons.

"Trying to annoy me is an act of avoidance mi hija. You can't run forever."

"I can try."

"So I see."

By November 2001 it was over a year since my incident with Mr.X and he was little more than a distant memory. My papers had been sorted and I was back in my misguided sense of security as I continued to ignore Andres and the supposed hole in my head. Then one day I was working when someone came running in with the news that the vice-president had just been assassinated. We quickly turned on the radio for an update, only to hear how his car had been blocked and snipers had opened fire. I listened in shock as they went on to name the two streets that met in a V-shape where the car had been obstructed. It was the corner where I lived, my apartment being situated above the shops at that precise point. The vice president's car had been stopped by another at the junction, people jumped out of that car and, with the help of snipers on the balcony of surrounding buildings, riddled the vice president's car with bullets.

As the news began to sink in, I was dealt the next blow as they announced one of the snipers (the main one) had been on the balcony of my apartment. My brain tried to compute all that this might mean. All I could think was that I needed to get back to the apartment as the police or military would surely break the door down. I have no idea what I thought I could do, I just knew I couldn't stay and do nothing. My fear in a great part due to the fact that in my apartment I had extensive documentation and transcripts from interviews regarding not only the dictatorship, but also commentaries on current politicians who had been actively involved in the dictatorship. I knew I had to remove all of this and had an obligation to protect those who had trusted me. With the support of a couple of friends we headed to the apartment and after lengthy questioning I was allowed to enter with ten soldiers in toll who proceeded to inspect the apartment and ensure I wasn't hiding any criminals. In the end they were content that the sniper had not come from my home as there was evidence that someone had climbed up one of the mango trees that surrounded the balcony and positioned themselves at a prime point to open fire. I was advised not to leave the country and to take care with my 'associations' and that supposedly was it. If only it were.

As soon as the police and military had left I filled three boxes with all the paperwork and cassettes I had in the house and drove straight to a courier's office, sending it all to the UK. It may have been an over reaction but the unpredictability of life and politics in Arajua ensured I was taking no risks.

The week that followed the vice-president's death came to be known by the press as 'Noviembre Arajua 2001 – *los siete días que conmovieron al Arajua*' (Arajua November 2001– The seven days that shook Arajua). As protesters gathered outside parliament, claims continued that the assassination was the work of a mafia movement aimed at destabilising the government. On the evening of the sixth day of the demonstrations, the electricity was cut in the capital, throwing the public square where people were gathered into total darkness. At this point snipers began randomly shooting into the gathered crowds. Over sixty people were acknowledged to have died while hundreds more were injured. Talks involving the military, the Church, Congress, the U.S. Embassy and the government brought about an agreement that led to the defusing of the near civil-war situation that had erupted. Heavily armed Brazilian commandos were sent in large numbers to Coronación to evacuate the now ex-president to the safety and luxury of Brazil, the same 'fate' Mendoza had enjoyed more than a decade earlier. The succession to the presidency fell, by law, to the hands of the parliamentary president, a man who, of course, had been a strong supporter of Mendoza.

As the week of demonstrations began, I opted to watch most of it from the relative safety of my home. Not least because my street now had military personnel standing guard including, for some strange reason, one permanently situated outside my apartment. He noted all my comings and goings in a notebook, as well as details of anyone who visited me and their car registrations.

One day however as I was watching the news, they announced there had been a breakthrough in the case and they had identified three of the snipers, their leader who, as it turned out, had been the one positioned on my balcony. They then showed his photograph and in that moment my world ground to a halt as I found myself staring at Mr.X.

On the one hand I was sure he chose that location deliberately, enjoying the upset and insecurity it would bring into my life. But on the other I'm not sure he was that scheming, or intelligent, in his thought processes. Who knows? Who cares? Well I did for a start. You see as Mr.X had begun the work on my documents for my identity card it meant his signature was also on a great deal of the paperwork therefore showing that I had an affiliation to him. To the police it either looked like a bizarre set of coincidences, or that I was somehow involved in the assassination. You couldn't make this stuff up if you tried. Honestly my ability to be in the wrong place at the wrong time is unsurpassable.

While the pride in and hopes for a new democracy that the demonstrations of that week had brought proved to be short-lived, my life took anew and interesting turn. The political crisis merely ended in a re-division of the spoils between the competing factions, and the masses of workers and peasants became more politically disenfranchised than ever. A decade after Mendoza's overthrow and the first tentative steps into a democratic climate, Arajua appeared to be heading into a new generation of revolutionary confrontation. I however remained in custody undergoing questioning on my 'involvement' in the assassination plot. It is not that the gravity of the situation was lost on me, but rather that the incredulity of the situation took over. I did not face my interrogation with bravery, but with disbelief. I did not brazenly refuse to answer their questions, I simply couldn't. I had not masterminded an assassination attempt although I couldn't help but think if I had I would have done a better job. You see at this point they had to let me go without charge because new information had been released.

Rumours had begun to circulate that the vice-president was actually already dead when he was shot at, having died of a heart attack in his lover's bed. And everyone who knew anything, or had seen anything, suddenly disappeared. Many apparently taking holidays from which they never returned. For once I felt immensely grateful that I knew nothing. Rumours spread that one of my neighbours had seen everything and told of how the military reached the scene before the police and ambulance, initially prohibiting the ambulance from entering the car and offering aid. The neighbour also told how when the vice-president's body was finally moved rigor mortis had already set in. My neighbour was never seen again. In my head I have chosen to believe he simply moved to a new house! ...and cut all contact with friends and family...and leave his job without warning...and...you get the picture.

Any thoughts of my possible involvement in the assassination quickly disappeared. Well not quickly enough to be honest. I was cleared, well 'more or less' as the Arajuans would say. Nothing is ever a straight 'yes' or 'no' there – it all falls into some very unclear shady place somewhere in the middle. An assassination that six years later was ironically confirmed to have been a sham; apparently the vice president had indeed died in the bed of his mistress and to cover up the scandal an elaborate assassination had been staged – a plan that not only led to the death of two innocent bodyguards and the chauffeur caught up in the cross fire when the car was shot at, but also led to riots and the deaths of so many innocent people caught up in what they believed to be a fight for democracy. The thing is in Arajua it is impossible to know the truth. Maybe the assassination was real, maybe not – we will never know the truth. And anybody who did know, as I said, seem to have mysteriously disappeared.

That was November 2001, I left Arajua the following year.

"Often we need to leave to find where we truly belong."

"Bloody hell Andres I really hope you're not implying I belong in Arajua!" I was horrified that he could ever imagine such a thing.

"Of course not," laughed Andres *"but it has forged you, for better or worse you must never forget that."*

Andres was right. I both love and hate Arajua. I am fiercely defensive if anyone tries to criticise it or its people. It's like your family, you are allowed to criticise them but you don't like it when someone else does it. I have learned that Arajua and I will always be linked no matter how hard I have tried to break free: it is part of who I have become.

I looked up at Andres as I spoke, "I don't think that is necessarily a bad thing."

I hope not anyway was my true thought.

XIV

When I came back to the UK, I returned to a country I no longer really knew and into which I certainly didn't seem to fit. I never expected to experience culture shock in the country of my birth. I needed to adapt and process many things and come to terms with the fact that those years of my life in South America are ones that I could never fully share – not because I don't want to but because there is no need to. After all how do you explain stories of black magic, holes in heads, torture victims and their torturers and assassinations? Whenever I did speak of my time there I was met with looks of incredulity. People don't know if I'm telling the truth or not. Sometimes I wonder myself.

"What is truth Andres?" I asked.

"A question that philosophers have grappled with for centuries and you want me to give you the answer?" Andres responded playfully.

"My memories changed over time and distance. Are the memories what actually happened?"

"That is irrelevant mi hija." I looked up at him surprised and confused by his response.

"But Andres they must be relevant, how can they not be?"

"Your emotions change, you change. The memories do not, but how you look at them, how you feel about them, of course that changes."

I thought about Andres' words. It was true. Far away from Arajua I had disengaged from the emotions that events had created in me. "But Andres it seems we live in two memories - the world's and our own. And the former always judges us."

"Be careful not to blame memory for poor judgement. Nothing sharpens the memory more than our futile attempts to forget."

"What's that supposed to mean?" I replied angrily, "What are you getting at?" I felt defensive despite not knowing why.

"Do not allow memory to diffuse facts. Learn how to sit with your memories. Befriend them," Andres paused as if he was going to say more but then changed his mind. He stood up and walked to the window and stared out for a while in silence. It was some moments before he spoke again, "Learn to treat your memories with compassion mi hija, and you will learn to understand yourself better."

Andres turned back to the window and I knew this signified the end of our conversation and the start of yet another riddle for me to solve.

It may seem odd to say in light of the stories I have shared, but in Arajua I never felt my safety was in question. There was an instinctive and inherent trust in all that I did and in all that occurred, a trust and an acceptance that this was part of my path. Safety is relative – relative to the situation, to the choices we make and to the risks we are willing to take. I will never tell all that happened in those years because telling will not change those events or make them disappear. Some things are not meant to be shared, but rather are intended to be guarded as dull memories in the confines of our mind. I will never tell all that happened because I no longer know what is true and what I have imagined. And if I do not pry into my own memories, I can convince myself that maybe, just maybe I imagined it all.

Over time I learned how to condense some stories into funny anecdotes and ignore the others. Or at least I tried. One thing I was determined to do was ignore the hole in my head. I was determined to believe no such thing existed. So I decided to embark on a journey of self-discovery, looking everywhere and anywhere for answers, so long as I never had to look inwards or deal with the hole in my head. As self-discoveries go, setting out with that in mind, I was destined to fail.

The main problem with journeys of self-discovery is what we actually discover and once on the trail it is hard to turn off and even harder, if not impossible, to turn back. You cannot erase from your memory what you have learned and continue your existence as before, much as you may want to at times. You can try of course, but the chances of success are limited. You are not the same person you were when you started out and the course of events in your life has adapted to this. There are so many moments in our lives, almost intangible, that shape a change in direction, a change in the formation of our personal history. If we could identify these moments at the time, our path would be a lot less rocky. But we so rarely do. I think I've always lived too much in my head; maybe that's the problem. The thing is that in my head everything always seems so much better. Only there do I have any hope of living up to my own expectations and only there are other people able to move freely within my space and get close to me. In reality everyone, including my own self, falls well short. That's the key problem, everyone is a disappointment sooner or later, and that includes me.

"Events shape us but that does not mean they define who you were and who you become."

"I think I'm afraid to face up to who I really am. Afraid of being this sin eater you tell me I am." Sometimes I think I feared my inability to meet Andres' expectations of me, even though he never spoke of having any.

"A dog bitten by a snake is afraid of sausages."

"What? Andres! I honestly think you make up these sayings and don't have any idea what they mean." I laughed.

185

"Take the meaning you choose from my words."

"That's a cop out."

"Is it? You left Arajua afraid. You took your fear with you and then couldn't understand why it had followed you."

I stared at Andres as the full weight of his words sank in. Had I really run from Arajua, carrying my fear? "Afraid? Of what?" I demanded.

"Afraid of the politics...of the history...of the stories you had heard...of not knowing what to do with what you had heard...of the responsibility...of the guilt...but most of all, of yourself. And you could not outrun yourself."

"I tried."

"And?"

"I'm still running."

"When will you learn? Like your shadow, you and your story are inseparable."

Ironically to avoid dealing with the hole in my head and any kind of spiritual path it may be leading me down, I went on a personal search through a myriad of spiritual beliefs. I was searching for a place where I could fit in, where I could belong. I know I should have started with my own skin! You name it I tried it: Tarot card readings, Angel card readings, Shamanic drumming, past life regression, meditation, Buddhism, Hinduism, New Age, Zen, Yoga, Paganism and the list goes on. I was never more disciplined in my life than during those three years I spent avoiding myself. I wanted answers and as I didn't like any that pointed me back to Arajua and the hole in my head, I kept looking. To be more precise, I kept avoiding. It was exhausting.

Every new spiritual angle brought a new 'mis' adventure and a confirmed awareness that I simply did not belong, but I immersed myself in it anyway. Actually no I didn't. everywhere I went I carried my baggage of cynicism, scepticism, anger and frustration. I found fault with every practice and everyone who was a part of it. Deep down I knew I would come back to Andres, but I was determined to fight it every inch of the way. Why? I really don't know.

"Because you were lost."
"No I wasn't." I responded defiantly.
"What is wrong with being lost mi hija? Why must you be so stubborn."
""I'm not stubborn and I'm not lost!"
"Mi hija, how can you be found if you are not lost?"

For a long time I threw myself into Buddhist meditation classes. "Threw" may be somewhat of an exaggeration, but I stuck it out longer than any of my other spiritual field trips. The class took place on a Monday night – the intention apparently being to set us in good stead for the rest of the week, calm and prepared for all that life might thrown our way. Right! On the first evening I looked around somewhat apprehensively at the others in the group, quickly feeling grateful that I had dragged a friend along. The plan being that I would talk only with her and nobody else would come near. Unfortunately I had brought the most sociable and talkative friend I had who immediately abandoned me to talk to everyone and anyone else. I concentrated on sending out my anti-social vibes – a warning that nobody should attempt to converse with me under any circumstances. In general it works quite well. Within five minutes I had scanned the room and judgmentally, and most uncharitably, summed up every person in it. But as I tried to meditate, based on very unclear instructions to do with clearing the mind, I was disturbed by the restlessness and sniffing of the drug addict in front of me, the tearfulness of the lost soul on my left and the groans and shuffling of the person to my right. Shamefully I must admit that my love for all sentient beings was failing before it had even begun. I felt no love for these people, only irritation, a sense of horror and, at the same time, a sense of arrogant relief that 'I wasn't like them'.

Whenever the tea break approached I tried to ensure that my body language clarified that there was a wall around me and that I had no desire to discuss the finer points of the meaning of life – particularly my life - with any of these people, or hear what I assumed would be their sad and desperate stories. I had of course decided that everyone in the room was sad and desperate, except for me and my friend, although her eager socialising and fascination with the Buddhists was beginning to make me wonder. The problem with sad, desperate people is that they are always clutching at other people and beliefs. They don't even realise that that is what they are doing because they assume that others must share their needs and interests. And I was too blind to see that that was exactly what I was doing! We are all clutching at something and I was really no different from them except in my arrogance. My sadness and desperation may have been less evident but it was there all the same. I wanted to see myself as 'superior' because I thought I was saner and healthier, but really we were all exactly the same.

The longer I studied meditation, the more the teachings became inextricable from Buddhism and the more of a conundrum I found myself in. So many of the teachings are similar to those of Christianity and those are easy to digest, from familiarity if nothing else. Digest is the wrong word – I can understand them in terms of what they are trying to say, that does not mean I have any desire to accept them. But then a shady area takes over in which my questioning increases and the answers steadily decrease. There always seems to be a silent nodding from the Buddhists at this point, the knowing nod that implies I will understand when I reach the right level. But how will I reach the right level without the understanding? And who says I want to be a part of their superior ranking? And how will I get the understanding if my questions remain unanswered? In Buddhism however, like in most faiths, there is never a straightforward answer to a straightforward question. The Buddhists just have a more infuriating approach to their lack of directness. Then the Buddhists would probably argue that there is no straightforward question because the answer lies inside! Or there is no answer because there is no question. What they don't realise is that if I truly embrace that it would lead me straight back to Andres.

I hate the smug superiority of so many of the 'knowing' on the spiritual path. They kindly but condescendingly pity those who haven't quite 'made it' yet, and who I'm sure they secretly think never will. So I am destined to keep turning around on my Samsaric wheel like an over-excited hamster, never quite attaining enlightenment. But if I ever should, I fully intend to move on rapidly to another spiritual plain – after all surely I will have earned it. The Buddhist concept of returning after enlightenment to help and guide other less enlightened souls, I find somewhat distressing. Perhaps on reaching enlightenment I will understand the value of this and eagerly embrace the idea. Perhaps. In the meantime, let darkness reign.

My initial meditation group was to last for three months but had individuals coming and going throughout according to their needs, breakdowns and outrages. I was relatively constant in my attendance, seduced by the thought of the tea and biscuits. We met each Monday evening where a room was rented in a large centre that played host to every kind of spiritual activity imaginable, many of which I had already tried. We would arrive and aid in the setting up of the room in which a yoga class had just ended. We would struggle to get up the narrow stairway as they pushed their way down complaining about our noisy chat throughout the last ten minutes of their class – their crucial period of calmness, relaxation and contemplation. At the top of the stairs we would try to find room to take off our shoes and coats without falling back down the stairs, as the yoga class tried to get theirs on. This power struggle continued every week. I am sure we won, being that we love all sentient beings and all that, and I am sure that all the good established from their yoga class was lost in those five minutes of battle for supremacy on the stairs. I enjoyed that thought every week.

A makeshift shrine of assorted pictures and bowls was set up, the incense and candles lit, the rug rolled out and the cushions positioned, the TV and video primed for the packaged teachings and, most importantly, the essentials laid out for the tea break. As the weeks progressed and we advanced to the chanting of mantras, a CD-player would be sought from the basement rapidly before the Zens, Shamanists, fairy followers, or other group of the moment got there first. Some days, waiting in the hallway before the group began, I would flick through the display of leaflets offering a myriad of ways to find one's inner self, methods of relaxation and de-stressing and a greater understanding of our being. There was something for every imaginable taste, and a few unimaginable ones also. The fairies I must say did intrigue me, but not enough to seek them out or join them. Apparently they can help your garden grow! I didn't have a garden. The more I saw of the other groups and the more I observed the people coming to participate in them, the more disturbingly normal my little Buddhist clique seemed and I looked forward to my Monday evenings of restful meditation, people-watching, tea and biscuits and general psychoanalysing of the mental status of those around me, few of whom were (in my expert opinion) stable. Undoubtedly Buddha would not have been impressed by my motives.

"The chicken sings what the cock teaches."
"I don't know what that means Andres but I'm sure it's an indirect criticism of me."

190

Andres laughed, "If I am going to criticise you, why would I be indirect?"

I had no answer for that. After all Andres was many things but, it was true, indirect was not one of them. I looked at him and burst out laughing.

"What amuses you so much?"

"Did the cock teach those chickens all my hopes and dreams so they could go singing in the hills?" We both laughed.

"I think they were too concussed." Andres replied with a cheeky grin.

"That's not funny Andres!"

Some weeks meditation class was more eventful than others. There was weeping, occasional heated debates, various problems of communication, the schizophrenic who, believing himself cured through enlightened spirituality, stopped taking his medication. His spiritual path was severely hindered by a disturbing confrontation between his opposing selves in an attack of paranoia on who was the more enlightened, followed by him being committed to a nearby psych ward. But in general things moved along calmly and the atmosphere was always pleasant in its own way. The only thing that disturbed me a little was the fact that nearly everyone in the room was called David, hence the need (and in my mind the justification) for clarification with nametags such as 'Junkie David', 'Abandoned David', 'Smug David' and on it went. I was definitely disturbed by the fact that Buddhism attracted all the 'Davids' within about a twenty-mile radius. I also realised that I would probably have been named 'Antisocial David'!

The format was the same for each meeting. After setting up we began with practise, followed by watching a short video instruction that was intended to lead to a discussion. At the end of the video the wary teacher would ask if there were any questions in a voice full of hope that none would actually be asked, or aggressively staring at myself or a couple of the others who almost always managed to find some point of query outside of the inevitable question: 'When's the tea break?' Actually it was me who usually asked that – well there are limits to how long you can sit in a meditative pose cutting off the blood supply to the lower half of your body. Those of us who asked questions usually ended up answering each other in an endless trail of ignorance festering upon even more ignorance and misguided conceptions. But we were content and felt something was being achieved. Who knows what though. When the teachers did become involved in our questioning and doubts, they appeared worn but satisfied with the brownie points the effort had no doubt earned them in their karmic standing. Once after my incessant and undoubtedly annoying questioning, the instructor said to me,

"Maya you are a clouded Buddha."

"What as opposed to a sunny one?"

"We are all Buddhas." He responded, choosing to ignore my sarcasm.

"Then why am I a clouded one?"

"You hinder your own enlightenment with your questions."

"I hinder my own enlightenment by wanting to understand?" This was clearly an indirect request for me to shut up. "Are you kidding me."

"Stop focusing on what I said. It is now in the past. When you are wrong admit it, when you are right be quiet."

I looked at the instructor trying to suppress my desire to punch his smug little face. But then came the eagerly awaited tea and biscuits. I am easily distracted. We would get up for the tea and as the blood slowly started to flow in our lower halves we would walk on numbed feet to get our tea, thud by thud like Frankenstein's monster. This was followed by more practise (occasionally interrupted by slurps of unfinished second cups of tea - that may have been me again).

Soon I grew tired of the meditation class as they looked for more commitment and I had grown tired of hiding there. I tried Shamanic drumming but that was short lived as it gave me a migraine. They told me it would induce a natural state of consciousness, whatever that means. Apparently it produces deeper self-awareness by inducing synchronous brain activity, integrating conscious and unconscious awareness. It didn't. I don't even know what that means. From there I wandered over to a guy who practiced past life regression therapy. I figured I could maybe try to find out if my head had been open in a previous life. The guy was weird, not in an Andres weird kind of way, but creepy and far too enthusiastic. He told me he was going to hypnotise me and then guide me through my previous lives. Now, over the years various people have tried to hypnotise me and none were successful. But I thought I'd let him try and was curious to see if it could really work.

He began by asking me to focus on a light and his monotonous voice. This went on far too long.

"You are starting to feel drowsy." He continued in his monotone.

I wasn't.

"Your eyelids are becoming heavier."

They weren't.

"You are feeling peaceful."

Not really.

"You will only respond to my commands."

I don't think so!

"You are now in a hypnotic state."

I wasn't.

He then asked me to focus in on a past life and began, somewhat unethically I'm sure, feeding me possibilities, a dangerous thing to do with my over-imaginative brain, so I started to go along with it and invent a story. All modesty aside it was rather good and we were both quite enthralled for a while. However his enthusiasm meant he was looking for more and clearly had no intention of bringing me out of my supposed hypnotic state. By this point not only had I lost interest, but I had also started running out of ideas and was now adapting (plagiarising) from a recent movie I had seen. Not knowing what else to do, I simply stopped talking. What I wanted to do was get up and leave, but as I was 'hypnotised' that was not a possibility. I was going to have to wait for him to bring me out of my hypnotic state. Unfortunately, the combination of my story being so detailed and fascinating, along with the fact that I was probably his first 'successful' case, meant he wasn't letting go easily. He began bombarding me with questions in an attempt to get me to continue the tales of my previous (albeit invented) life and all I could do was stay silent in the hope he would give up. I even started dozing off at one point, however his incessant questioning with his monotone voice made that impossible. Still he would not give up and tried to rouse me back to speaking without going so far as to bring me out of my hypnotic state.

"What happened next?" he asked enthusiastically.

Silence.

"Did you escape with the crown?"

Please don't ask me where I was going with the storyline, let's just call it creative license.

"No..no…" I cried dramatically. I was rapidly running out of ideas and that was the best I could come up with.

"What is it - tell me? What's happening?"

Silence.

"Tell me your true identity? You can trust me." This guy was crazier than I thought and if there was one thing I knew for sure, it was that he could not be trusted.

"No, no - the pain! It's too much!" I had no idea where I was going with this except hopefully out the front door.

"Pain! Pain? What are they doing to you? Tell me!" Unfortunately I seemed to have piqued his interest even further, if that was possible.

"They're going to kill me. I know too much. They know...they know..." I had no idea what they knew.

"What? Tell me! What did...."

"The pain! Make it stop! I'm begging you." I shouted cutting him off. Did this guy have no ethics?

"Tell me..."

"Baby Jesus!" Where the hell did that come from?

"What?"

My story had taken a new turn that neither of us had seen coming.

"Baby Jesus..." I repeated.

"What?"

"He knows. He knows...." I have no doubt Baby Jesus is well aware of my childhood theft, however I had no intention of bringing it up and had no idea why those words had come out of my mouth. Desperation perhaps, however over the years I have learned that Baby Jesus has a dark sense of humour and in my moments of need when I turn to him, I'm sure he takes great delight in watching me try to extricate myself from the impossible situations I inadvertently place myself in.

"Baby Jesus. I can't take it any more...Stop! Stop! I can't do this anymore. Please stop!"

"But I...." Was this man ever going to give up?

"STOP! No! It's too late..." I shouted followed by a very impressive blood curdling scream which scared the living daylights out of the idiot. I added another for good measure. He quickly 'brought me round', adding that I would remember nothing of our session and feel calm and rested. I don't think so! He was extremely eager to make further appointments as I had been such an excellent candidate for regression therapy and hypnosis he explained. I agreed to another session the following week. Needless to say I never returned.

In order to avoid that damn hole in my head, I put myself in so many ridiculous situations over and over again. Entertaining as many were (retrospectively at any rate) they were also exhausting.

"Maya you do not need to become the victim of what goes on in your mind."

"Victim! Nice choice of word."

"Mi hija, the main root of all our suffering is not knowing who we really are. Our fabrications exist because we give them credibility."

"I don't understand." I had no intention of trying to understand and I didn't like where the conversation was heading.

"You will find it inside of you. You have it inside – you just need to learn how to look for it."

I tried to decide if the look on Andres' face was one of frustration or pity. If I had asked he would have said neither of course. *"Am I such a bad student?"*

Andres laughed heartily, *"So now she's my student!"*

"I never was a good student." I offered conciliatorily.

"Stop seeking knowledge and you will become better." He grinned that irritating grin when he knew he had said something I couldn't quite grasp.

"Are you sure you're not some kind of Buddhist monk with all this there is no answer because there is no question crap!"

"Don't be disrespectful…and perhaps I was once, in another life."

"You're doing it again. It really does not help."

"I don't ask you to believe Maya. I never have. You will find your own belief, that's what makes you an individual."

"I know, not following everyone else like a sheep. Having the courage to roar like a lion...when the time and the circumstances are right of course."

Andres grinned widely, "So you do listen sometimes."

"Listening and understanding are not the same thing." I replied smugly.

"That is true, again proof you have listened." He was enjoying himself, playing with me had almost become a past time. "And retaining is another, and still your weakest point."

"That's unfair!" I protested vehemently, hurt by what I assumed to be a judgment of my failure.

"I am not judging you. Don't be so serious mi hija, judgments are for fools, fools and judges if there is a difference." Yet again he knew my thoughts before I had spoken them aloud. I often wondered if he read my mind or if I was such an open book, so obvious and basic in my reactions and assumptions. The ego in me hoped it was the former! "And failure is not a concept I believe in, everything is about learning."

"Learning with no knowledge?" I tried to catch him out with my sarcastic response, I should have known better.

"Excellent! Indeed you are learning. Learning, listening and retaining, perhaps there is hope for my little student yet."

Even at the times I wanted to be angry at Andres I simply couldn't. He frustrated the hell out of me, I couldn't deny that. All his half answers or non-answers, telling me to look within, his knowing smiles – all of them grated on me. Yet he always made me smile in the end, always helped me find some peace.

"Smile mi hija," continued Andres, "don't let yesterday consume too much of today."

XV

For the last three years it feels like I have been trying to live different lives. I laugh when people say they know me. They know nothing but what I have allowed them to know and I engineer that well. It's not that I don't like people but I do compartmentalise my life. There are people I know in different settings and so they know different sides of me and different things about me. That's the way I like it: no crossing over and keep everyone at arm's length. Many thought I had the perfect life; people were even envious of me. That made me laugh. The truth is I was doing a juggling act to fill every moment of every day just so I didn't think too much. I would go to bed at night exhausted and tell myself 'tomorrow I will make time to think, tonight I just need to get some sleep'. Of course every day was the same so there was never that time to stop and think.

"How much I fear that no one but you will see the potential in me...the worth."

"Your worth is inside of you. Don't look outside for approval."

"Easier said than done."

"Don't be swayed by others' criticism or praise. Ultimately it means nothing. It does not make you who you are. Their praise and acceptance will not make you better; their criticism and rejection will not make you worse."

"It's not that simple."

"Nothing of value ever is."

"But..."

"You want others to see your worth, but you can't even see it yourself."

My vague attempts at spirituality of any kind had brought me back to where I had started. They always did. I had heard of an old Spanish woman who spoke to angels and decided to visit her. I wasn't sure what I believed (it seems I never am), but I liked the concept and I decided to visit her. I desperately wanted answers even though I had long since run out of questions. She lived in an old cottage on the outskirts of town so I took a bus as close as I could to where she lived. It should have been a short journey but the bus took a winding route, passing bus stops where nobody was waiting. Those on the bus had almost all disembarked at previous stops before I reached mine. I then followed the map a friend had scribbled on a napkin in a coffee shop a couple of days before. It didn't take long to find the house which looked like it had seen better days. I smiled as I looked at it, remembering the first time I had visited Andres.

When she opened the door, she looked at me surprised, as if she recognised me. I looked back equally surprised as I was sure I too had seen her before. And then she laughed. It couldn't be! It was impossible. Her laugh was exactly the same as that toothless old woman who always sat in the rocking chair at Andres' house. But that was years ago, she couldn't possibly still be alive? And how could she be here thousands of miles away? I knew it couldn't possibly be her but the similarities were unnerving.

"Welcome mi hija, come in, come in." 'Mi hija' she had said. How was that possible `I thought but then quickly told myself it was a common Spanish expression and I was reading too much into it. Or was I? She smiled as she beckoned me into her home, directing me to the kitchen. Strangely I felt immediately at ease.

"How have you been mi hija?"

What a strange question I thought, why wouldn't she ask, "How are you?" Her question implied we had met before. "Excuse me but do I know you?" I asked hesitantly.

"Why are you so sad?" she asked ignoring my question.

"I'm not sad." I lied. She looked up at me and smiled. "Have we met before?" I tried again.

"Tea?" She asked, already laying out two cups. I nodded, waiting for her to answer my question or ask why I was here. She didn't and we sat in silence drinking our tea.

"Have we met before?' I asked again breaking the silence.

She laughed. "We share some friends in common. One is standing behind you. Do not be afraid, he is embracing you. Some call them spirits, some call them angels…some even call them shadows." The old woman looked at me and chuckled the way Andres would often do. "His wings are wrapped tightly around you; he wants to comfort you through your pain." I was starting to feel uncomfortable and was resisting the urge to make a joke about having another egun in the hope that she would stop talking. "He has always been with you mi hija, always protecting, always loving. He has a message for you." I looked at her dubiously as she took a deep breath before her next words. "He says the red shoes were beautiful and he's sorry he was not strong enough to tell you that day."

Tears began rolling down my face. The tears became sobs, uncontrollable exhausting sobs. Years of holding in the pain, years of my 'mis' adventures to seek answers I then refused to accept, years of running, they had all led me to this moment. It was one of those childhood moments that I thought could never be returned to. Moments to be left well alone in that sacred space where we know that imaginary friends are real and angels sit on our shoulders and whisper in our ears, kissing the strands of our hair that blow in the wind. Sometimes, on good days, I think I still hear those whispers and feel the gentle kisses and I reach out my hand and grasp at the air and hear their laughter as they run to join the shadows in world that exists astride mine.

You may wonder still why I accepted her words, why I believed without question. I'm not even sure that the answers are relevant anymore, although I understand why you may want them. All I know is that this day was the culmination of many in which the presence of angels around me was something of which I was forced to become aware.

"When you feel alone mi hija, turn to your shadow, your grandfather walks with you there."

When I left the old woman's house that day, I had found a peace that had been lacking. I knew the running had stopped. I had spent three years running, avoiding the inevitable. When I finally stopped long enough I knew what I had to do. After so many years I picked up the phone not sure what to expect.

"Andres?"

"Mi hija." He remembered me. Immediately I felt his warmth, his patience. "I've been waiting."

"How did you know I would call?"

"How do I know the sun will rise every morning?" Andres replied with that laugh I knew so well. "I see that the shadows beckon, whispering their stories, awaiting the listener."

"Yes. I think it's time."

"I look forward to seeing you mi hija." And with that he hung up. There was nothing more to say.

Andres knew I had made the decision to return. I wanted to confront my demons, do things on my terms. I wanted to stop running. To do so I knew I had to return one last time.

I am not the hero of this story. Simply I was someone often in all the wrong places at all the right times. There was a point I would have said at the wrong time, but I can see that was not the case. Everything that happened was a part of the path that was mine to walk. I have been fortunate, although at times that fortune was misplaced. I wasn't lucky and it wasn't some kind of adventure. It was simply the life I led and luck - good or bad - never figured in that. I wish I could say I became some kind of revolutionary due to all that happened in Arajua, that I could take the credit for being a brave and amazing person, but that is not the truth and it was never like that. My mettle was never truly tested so I will never know and when I look at people like Alberto, I respect and admire them so much and know that I am so far from that kind of achievement as a human being.

As I sat in the back of the taxi on the way to the airport, I thought about how sometimes when you are driving and look out the window, up at the sky or out at the countryside, you realise that every place looks much the same. It could be the same sky, the same hills and trees – none of it holds any sense of ownership, of 'belonging'. And I often wonder, if I didn't know where I was, where would I actually be. The only answer I ever seem to find is 'anywhere but here'. So now as I look out of the car window I see the trees and the sky, there's a certain atmosphere, a certain view and as darkness comes there's something familiar about it all. Buildings have a familiar air, an air that has a familiar colour and smell. And there is a reflection coming from the sea, from the invisible colours on the horizon. In Coronación that line is the greenish blue mist of the Chaco and here it is the greenish blue mist that comes with the winter air early in the morning. In the end they are all one and the same. In the end our stories follow us wherever we go.

When I finally stepped off the plane in Arajua I was confident that I would finally get that closure I longed for.

How wrong could I have been?

Printed in Great Britain
by Amazon